Haunted High Book 5

Ashes of Night

By Cheree Alsop

ISBN: 9781986668163
Cover Design by Robert Emerson
Editing by Sue Player
www.ChereeAlsop.com

To my husband,
I want to live where you live, even if that means we're both ghosts.
To my children,
Each story I write is for you.

To the reader holding this book,
You are unique, you are your own kind of beautiful,
And you make this world better just by being a part of it.
Never give up.

ALSO BY CHEREE ALSOP

The Haunted High Series-

The Wolf Within Me
The Ghost Files
City of Demons
Cage the Beast
Ashes of Night

The Silver Series-

Silver
Black
Crimson
Violet
Azure
Hunter
Silver Moon

The Werewolf Academy Series-

Book One: Strays
Book Two: Hunted
Book Three: Instinct
Book Four: Taken
Book Five: Lost
Book Six: Vengeance
Book Seven: Chosen

Heart of the Wolf Part One
Heart of the Wolf Part Two

The Galdoni Series-

Galdoni
Galdoni 2: Into the Storm
Galdoni 3: Out of Darkness

The Small Town Superheroes Series-

Small Town Superhero
Small Town Superhero II
Small Town Superhero III

Keeper of the Wolves
Stolen
The Million Dollar Gift
Thief Prince
When Death Loved an Angel

The Shadows Series

Shadows- Book One in the World of Shadows
Mist- Book Two in the World of Shadows

The Monster Asylum Series

Book One- The Fangs of Bloodhaven
Book Two- The Scales of Drakenfall

Girl from the Stars

Book 1- Daybreak
Book 2- Daylight
Book 3- Day's End

Book 4- Day's Journey
Book 5- Day's Hunt

The Pirate from the Stars

The Dr. Wolf Series

Book 1- Shockwave
Book 2- Demon Spiral
Book 3- The Four Horsemen
Book 4- Dragon's Bayne

The Prince of Ash and Blood

The Game Breaker Series
Book 1- Pawn

Chapter One

"SOMETHING'S FOLLOWING US."

The strange voice woke me. At the feeling of the bag over my head and my hands cuffed in front of me, I kept perfectly still.

"What is it?"

"It looks like a vampire."

"Why is a vampire following us?"

"How do I know? I didn't think vampires could run so fast."

They sounded tense. I bided my time. My head ached. I tried to remember what had brought me there. I remember returning to the Academy and stopping a fight between Uncle Conrad and Professor Briggs. When I went to bed, Alden had been missing. I tracked him down and he told me about Sparrow flying away. The thought of the baby sylph dragon lost somewhere in the city gripped my heart. I willed my breathing to slow as I fought to remember.

I had laid on my bed and was just about asleep when hands grabbed me in the dark. Someone threw the bag over my head. I remembered a threat.

"Move and die," someone had whispered into my ear.

I grabbed him and threw him over my shoulder, then something hit the back of my head. At least my headache made sense.

"Drive faster."

"I am driving faster!"

"Maybe I can shoot him. Hold on."

The sound of a zipper was followed by the metallic click of clip sliding into a gun. It was a sound I knew all too well. The person to the right of me rolled down his window. That meant the driver sat in front of me. A quick check showed fast breathing from the front seat. There was something different to their scent, something I had smelled only once before. My heart sped up at the realization that I was surrounded by werewolves.

"Steady," the man in the driver's seat commanded. "That's it. A little closer."

If Vicken was the one following the car, I couldn't let him get shot.

"No!" I shouted.

I threw my bound hands over the driver's head and pulled. He gave a strangled yell. I felt the car jerk to the left, then to the right. The car struck something that sent us flipping through the air.

I didn't know if it was worse watching us roll or experiencing it with a bag covering my eyes. My back slammed into the roof and then I fell back to the seats while my companions bounced around me. I wondered if any of them had thought to wear a seatbelt. If they had put one on me when

I was unconscious, I wouldn't have been able to reach the driver. I figured being in the middle of rolling to a stop wasn't the time to preach vehicle safety.

The car finally halted on its hood. With my body twisted and upside down, I managed to shove the bag away. It was night and the car lights had gone out during the crash. I took advantage of the darkness to kick out the glass on my side.

"Where do you think you're going?" the person beside me demanded with a groan.

I ignored him and wiggled my way through the window. I was about to stand when a hand grabbed my arm with a grip of steel.

"Finn, are you alright?"

I grinned at Vicken's worried expression. His fangs glowed in the moonlight. The accident had landed us down a slight hill from the road. No other cars were in visible. I rolled my shoulders to check for damage. I would have bruises, but nothing worse.

"I'm harder to kill than that."

"Tell me about it," he replied drily. "I—"

Vicken jerked backwards with a hand on his shoulder. The sound of a gunshot rang out.

"Wait!" I shouted. I threw myself in front of the vampire. He fell to his knees. I looked back to see one of the werewolves stand up from his hiding place behind the car.

"That should hold him," he said with a satisfied nod.

I launched myself at the werewolf. He backed up several steps in surprise at my attack. I hit him so hard he landed on his back. My hands closed around his throat.

"I was doing you a favor!" he said tightly. "The vampire was going to kill you!"

"The vampire is my friend," I growled.

His eyes widened. "Th-that changes things."

"That was a good shot."

I looked back to see another werewolf standing over Vicken. He carried a gun that matched the one that had shot my friend.

"Stay away from him!" I shouted.

I grabbed the gun the werewolf beneath me still held, rolled to the right to break it from his hand, then rose to a knee with the gun aimed at the man near Vicken.

He quickly held up his hands.

"Whoa, slow down, son. We're here to help."

I glared at him, "Step away from my friend."

His eyebrows rose at my reference to Vicken, but he did as he was told.

"He'll be fine," he said. He waved his gun with his hands still up. "It's a stunner. No big deal. He'll wake up with a headache. That's about it."

The nonchalance to his words after seeing my friend go down made red burn in my vision. I shot him and then shot the werewolf next to me in the chest. Both dropped the way Vicken had. I ran to my friend and checked his pulse. I sighed in relief at the feeling of his heartbeat beneath my fingers.

"Let's get you out of here," I told Vicken.

I knelt and picked him up in my arms. It wasn't an easy feat given the manacles around my wrists, but I managed. The sound of cars pulling off the road made me hurry.

"If we can just find somewhere to hide until you wake up—"

"What's going on here?"

The woman's voice was gruff and deep. I turned slowly and glanced up the hill. Four men stood on either side of a middle-aged woman wearing green cargo pants and a brown shirt. All had guns trained on us. Even with the one I held in my hand beneath Vicken's legs, I didn't have a chance. Firing uphill and unable to aim would be a losing battle at best.

I watched her carefully, aware that the sight of the two fallen werewolves behind me didn't bode well for the encounter. Even though I was downhill and couldn't smell them, the moonlight that reflected off of their gazes let me know they were also werewolves. I didn't have time to be amazed that I was currently surrounded by more werewolves than I had ever encountered in my life; my friend's wellbeing was literally in my hands. I had to play it smart.

"They kidnapped me. I don't take kindly to being kidnapped," I said levelly.

The woman's expression was calculating when she replied, "I think there's been a misunderstanding. My pack was on a rescue mission." She crossed her arms. I glimpsed what looked like the head of a wolf branded on her forearm.

I shook my head. "Rescue should be willing, don't you think? And they shot my friend. That doesn't sound like a rescue to me."

The woman gave a shallow nod. "I'm afraid some procedures may not have been followed accurately. They'll be held accountable for their actions."

"I'd like to return to the Academy," I told her.

A glimmer of surprise showed in her eyes. "The Academy doesn't allow werewolves."

"It does now," I replied. "And as far as I knew, I was the only one." I gave the men with her a searching glance.

Her lips pulled up in the barest hint of a smile. "Our secrecy is our protection. I'm just sorry we had to meet this way."

"Me, too," I began. "But—"

The snap of a twig warned me a second too late. I spun and fired. My bullet went wide at the same time that one impacted high on my sternum. Numbness flowed instantly through me. I fell to my knees, then collapsed on top of Vicken.

"Sorry," I mumbled as my eyes closed.

Hands grabbed my arms and pulled me away from Vicken.

"See those fangs? And the werewolf's friends with the vampire. I'm not so sure about this," a male voice said.

"Look at the mess he made. Are you sure he's worth it?"

"This certainly isn't going the way I planned," the woman said. "Get him back to the Den."

"What about the vamp?"

"We'll have to take him with us."

"We should leave him here to die of thirst. That's what he deserves for attacking us," a man suggested gruffly.

The woman's voice was heavy when she said, "No. We'll keep him under. We don't need another fiasco like the winter slaughter."

"He'll need blood."

"We'll cross that bridge when we get to it."

"What about the car?" someone else asked.

"Burn it," the woman ordered.

I was set in the back of another vehicle. Though I couldn't get my eyes to open, my brain refused to slide into unconsciousness. I wondered if I was actually getting used to being shot. Perhaps I had built up some sort of tolerance. I wasn't especially sure that was a good thing, but maybe I could use it to my advantage.

By the time we stopped, I had heard references to the Den several times as well as grumbling about some sort of gauntlet.

"You would do better if you learned to keep your nose down and your thoughts wolf," a man suggested.

"Just because you think like an animal doesn't mean it's easy for the rest of us," the one who was whining replied.

"Quiet," the woman said. "You're lucky you passed the trial; it's a lot more difficult than when you ran it. Keep this up and another year of rounds will be the least you deserve."

"Yes, Meg," they both replied sullenly.

Silence filled the car. I preferred it with the way my head was starting to pound.

The car finally stopped. I heard the driver shift in his seat as if he was anxious to leave.

"I'm getting as far away from that vampire as I can," he muttered. "He stinks like dirt and blood."

"You just volunteered to take him to the holding room," Meg replied in her deep voice. "Jax, help Bruno. Make sure the chains are tight. Stix, you're in charge of this werewolf. Roundy and Gets, carry in Cooper and Devin." She paused, then said, "I can't believe he got the drop on them wearing handcuffs. That's ridiculous. Tell them they get rounds when they wake up."

"Even with the headaches?" someone asked.

"Maybe it'll teach them a lesson," Meg replied.

Someone picked me up and swung me over his shoulder like a sack of potatoes. I hung with my head down his back and my handcuffs in front of me as he carried me in that graceful position into wherever we had ended up.

"Put a manacle around his neck."

"What?" the man carrying me questioned with surprise in his voice.

"You heard me," Meg replied. "Manacle him and put another chain on those handcuffs. It's either that or the cage. I don't need him phasing and attacking our pack because he's mad about the vampire. We need whatever control we can get until some ground rules are covered."

"Yes, Meg."

I was set on a hard surface. The sound of keys caught my ear. I heard metal slide on metal and knew they were close to using the manacle.

I had survived a manacle in the Mythic Labs. The pressure of the metal band and death by strangulation if I tried to phase had nearly overwhelmed me with the claustrophobia. I refused to fall under someone's power like that again.

I forced my eyes open and pushed to my feet. "Don't touch me," I growled.

The werewolf closest to me backed off with a shout of surprise. I felt a wall against my back and leaned against it for support in the hopes that my blinding headache wouldn't get the best of me. I stood in a hallway of sorts made of huge bricks. Sound echoed from the matching brick floor to the high ceiling that was nearly lost in the shadows. It looked as though I was in the middle of a medieval castle, but that made no sense.

"Take it easy," Meg said. Her arms were folded across her chest and she regarded me with a hint of frustration in her steely green eyes. Her gray-streaked blonde hair was pulled back in a ponytail and from this close, I could see the deep lines around her eyes and mouth along with a scar that ran from her jaw down her neck and was lost beneath her shirt.

"Where's Vicken?" I demanded.

"Safe," she replied.

I glared at her. "Not safe enough. You need to let us go."

Other men and women began gathering behind Meg. By their scents they were all werewolves. The fact amazed me.

Meg shook her head. "You're not going anywhere for a long time. You might as well get used to it."

"You can't keep me here," I said through gritted teeth.

She gestured to the thick handcuffs around my wrists. "You're in no position to make demands."

A few chuckles came from the werewolves behind her. The adults I saw had the same wolf head brand on their forearms as Meg. She silenced them with a glance.

I tried a different route. "You said werewolves aren't welcome at the Academy, but I've been just fine there."

"Oh, really?" Meg replied. "No prejudice? No wary glances as though they're afraid you're going to kill someone?" She nodded at the embarrassed look I couldn't quite stifle. "They're waiting for you to mess up, and when you do, they'll kill you. It's what they do."

I shook my head quickly. "They wouldn't kill me."

"Oh yeah? What about Conrad Roe? They killed him quickly enough."

Relief made me smile. "Conrad's not dead! In fact, he's at the Academy right now. He went back to help us!"

Talking began behind Meg. She glanced back and then at me again. "What are you talking about?"

"Conrad's not dead," I repeated. "He survived. But a demon controlled him, which is why Vicken and I need to return to the Academy. We killed Conrad's demon, but we have to go after Chutka. It's the only way."

Meg shook her head. "You're not making any sense. Conrad's dead. They framed him after vampires murdered other students. They wanted to keep werewolves out, so fear was the best way to do it."

I shook my head quickly. "That's not true at all! You need to let me go. We have to get back!"

"What you have to do is calm down and settle in. You're going to be here for quite some time," Meg replied.

"I can't." I looked around for anything I could use as leverage. The other werewolves were watching me as though I was either crazy or unstable. Their wary expressions calmed me faster than anything Meg could have said. I was used to being careful around dangerous expectations. The Academy had given me plenty of practice. I took a steeling breath.

"I'm calm," I told her. "But I need you to understand that it's urgent for me to return to the Academy. They need my help."

A man behind her chuckled. "Like mythics would take assistance from a werewolf."

I stared at him. "Of course they would. We're mythics, too."

Laughter rolled through the crowd at my words.

Meg held up a hand to silence them, but a humored smile showed on her face when she said, "Werewolves are werewolves. Mythics are their own creatures. We aren't the same."

I opened my mouth to argue, but she cut me off. "Do you know of any mythics that change form the way we do? How about werewolves who can perform magic? Or mythics that have animal survival instincts? What about pack hierarchy? Do you think mythics follow the same rules engrained in our nature since the beginning?"

I grabbed onto her comment about pack hierarchy. "I'm an Alpha."

Her brow furrowed and she watched me for a moment before laughter bubbled again from her. "Son, what makes you think you're an Alpha?"

Her question caught me by surprise. "Well, uh, I just am."

Her eyebrows rose. "Why? Because some night owl running the Academy told you so? What does she know?"

I was at a loss for words.

Reading my expression, Meg motioned to one of the men who stood protectively on either side of her. "Stix, remove his handcuffs."

The man stared at her. "Are you serious?"

She nodded. "He doesn't need them."

I felt her gaze on me when the werewolf approached. I fought the urge to back off before he could touch me and instead held my ground. His nervous expression kept me still while he slid the key into the thick handcuffs and unlocked them. When the handcuffs were off, I rubbed at my wrists to encourage the circulation to return to my hands.

"What's your name?" Meg asked.

"Finn," I answered. I didn't feel like they deserved my entire name. I kept it to myself to pretend as though I at least had some control over the situation. Besides, if they had been told lies about Conrad and the Academy, I didn't want to think they believed lies about my mother. I wouldn't give them the chance to disgrace her memory.

"Come with me, Finn," Meg replied. "I want to show you something."

The crowd parted to let us pass. Their gazes bored into my back as though they seldom saw werewolf strangers. A glance back showed six of them following. A shiver ran down my spine. I returned my attention to where we were going.

"It's not a kind life out there for a werewolf," Meg said conversationally as she led me down the long hallway. Other halls branched off from the one we walked, but she kept us moving forward. She glanced at me. "You're lucky you survived out there."

I figured telling her the truth wouldn't hurt anything and might be enlightening. I had gone so long without any information about werewolves other than what I could figure out for myself that I was willing to show a little patience as long as Vicken wasn't in danger.

"I didn't know I was a werewolf until I phased after an accident."

She nodded. "Many of us phase for the first time due to extreme circumstances." She met my gaze. "It must have been hard doing so all alone."

The understanding in her eyes was something I hadn't expected. I cleared my throat and said, "It was a surprise. My mother died when I was younger and my dad's werewolf gene remained dormant. He didn't know much about being a werewolf."

That last line was an understatement. The amount of knowledge either of us had about werewolves could have fit on a sticky note.

As if she guessed I was making light of the situation, Meg gave me a kind smile. "You've made it this far on your own. That's saying something. We could definitely use a werewolf like you here."

"Where are we?" I asked.

We had neared the end of the hallway. It opened up into a wide space that smelled heavily of the musky earth scent of many werewolves.

"Let me show you," Meg replied.

When we reached the opening, my mouth dropped. Meg grinned at me and said, "Welcome to the Den."

The hallway turned into a ramp that wound down several stories around the outside of the huge cavern. Tunnels lit by warm glowing lights branched away at regular intervals. At the bottom, at least the size of a football field, was an enormous open area where children played on playground equipment while men and women ate and chatted. Teenagers occupied one section where the entire wall appeared to be taken up by game screens and computers.

"Are those all werewolves?" I asked in shock.

Meg nodded. "Dormant or active. Both are welcome at the Den." She motioned toward the children. "You can understand our need for secrecy. I apology for your rough treatment. We have a lot to keep safe here."

"I understand," I replied. And I did. I had fought so hard to protect my friends and the students at the Academy. If anyone could comprehend the drive to keep those who needed it from harm, I did.

Meg nodded at the men behind me. "We're fine here, gentlemen. Thank you for your help."

"Keep your gun out," the man named Stix suggested when he walked past her.

Meg rolled her eyes. "You worry too much."

"That's my job," Stix replied before he headed down the ramp after the others.

We watched as two young children detached from the group and ran up to hug him.

"His wife was killed during a misunderstanding with a vampire coven," Meg told me. "He's raising his children on his own." She met my gaze. "I'm telling you this so you'll understand why he's so rough around the edges. He's been there." Her gaze narrowed thoughtfully and she said, "I think you've been there, too." Her face took on a motherly cast. "You're a bit young to carry so many worries on your shoulders."

I didn't know how to reply to that. I definitely hadn't expected any kindness or understanding from my kidnappers. It unsettled me.

"I want you to go down there and see how things are before you judge us too harshly," Meg said. "Maybe you'll understand why we've hidden away from the world."

I asked the question that wouldn't allow me to lower my walls. "What about Vicken?"

She watched me carefully, her expression guarded. "Is that your vampire friend?"

I nodded. "My best friend. I'm responsible for what happens to him here, and I need to know he's alright."

She considered this before she said, "You know that vampires and werewolves are natural enemies?"

"I do," I replied. I gave her a wry smile. "It's something we've had to address a few times, but we've managed to survive it."

That made an answering smile touch her lips. She said, "Your vampire friend will come to no harm. He's currently being kept in a safe room in a state of controlled unconsciousness." At my worried look, she said, "Don't worry. He is safe. It's the first time I've ever protected a vampire here, and I'm sure the Pack will have something to say about it, but you have my word."

"Thank you," I told her. I walked toward the ramp.

"Oh, one more thing," Meg said.

I turned to face her.

"There are no Alphas in the Den."

"Why not?" I asked in surprise.

Her gaze held mine when she replied, "Because there are no more Alphas left in the world."

Chapter Two

HER LAST WORDS REMAINED at the forefront of my mind as I made my way down the ramp. By the stares that greeted me from children and adults alike, word of my presence had already flooded through the Den. I walked down the path that led from the playground to a lounge area filled with werewolf adults watching football, soccer, and what looked like a singing competition. The looks of distrust I met warred with the occasional smile. I made sure to keep my gawking at a minimum but they didn't bother to do the same. Talking rose the moment I left any area; my cheeks heated at references to 'the vampire protector', and statements like 'he must be dangerous' and 'we can't trust him'.

At one point, a girl with silver and pink streaked hair broke the mold of gossip and distrust when she waved me over to join a heated foosball competition.

"Come play," she invited.

The looks of the other teenage werewolves weren't nearly as happy, but they moved over to make room, leaving me the position of goalie.

"It's been a while since I played," I told them nervously.

To be honest, the last time I had played a game of foosball was with Sebastian and Drake at the Cleary Recreation Center about two years ago. The thought of Bast laughing when he slammed a goal past Drake's goalie gave me a pang of sadness.

Distracted by my thoughts, I let the ball slide by without blocking it.

"Nice move," one of the werewolves said. He had dark skin and matching eyes. By the way the other teenagers looked at him, he was in charge. "Way to not do anything."

"Sorry," I mumbled.

The girl with the streaked hair threw me an apologetic look.

"Why don't you use your Alpha skills to tell us how to play?" the teenager continued.

"Yeah," one of his friends piped in. "What Rhett said. Make us lose, Alpha. That'd be proof."

The others burst out laughing.

"I don't know what you're talking about," I said. I heard my sullen tone, but couldn't help it.

The first boy grinned, showing a gap between his front teeth. "You know, compel us. You say you're an Alpha. Prove it."

I shook my head. "I don't know how."

They laughed again.

The girl glared at her friends. "Shut up, you guys."

Rhett glared at her in return. "You're the one who invited the freak over here, Kiyah."

Her eyes narrowed. "I thought you'd have a shred of decency toward a newcomer."

"You thought wrong," Rhett spat.

She launched herself at him.

I could only stare in shock as she knocked him to the ground and jumped on him with her fists flying. Rhett kicked her off. She stumbled backwards. He lunged to his feet and bowled her over.

The teenage werewolves around me didn't interfere. A circle formed around the pair as they brawled. Cheers for each side rose.

"Teach her a lesson, Rhett!" one of the boys said.

"Hit him again, Kiyah!" several girls shouted.

Kiyah appeared to be holding her own for a moment, then Rhett swept her legs and she landed hard on her back. He slammed a fist into her cheekbone with enough force that her head rebounded off the floor. Before he could land another one, I shoved through the crowd and grabbed his arm.

"Let go of me, loser!" he growled.

"She's had enough," I replied. "Leave her alone."

His eyes narrowed. Kiyah's expression showed her shock at my interference. Already, a bruise was forming on her cheek where he had hit her.

"Only curs interfere," Rhett said. "Let me go!"

"Only bullies pick on girls," I shot back, refusing to release his arm.

"What's going on here?"

The werewolves quickly parted and my heart fell when Stix was revealed. He didn't look pleased to see me there, but when his gaze shifted from me to Rhett who was still crouched over Kiyah, anger simmered in his eyes.

"Explain yourself, Rhett."

Rhett shrugged out of my grip and rose quickly. "Kiyah started it," he said. "She's defending the cur."

I held out my hand to the girl. She glared at me and swatted my hand to the side before rising on her own.

"Thanks a lot," she grumbled.

Stix glared at me. "If your goal in coming here was to create trouble, you've done it."

"I didn't ask to come here," I shot back. "I was kidnapped, remember?"

He crossed his arms. "The werewolves here are grateful to be safe."

"Well, I'm not," I replied. "I was safe before they dragged me here. Show me where my friend is and I'll gladly leave."

Gasps and whispers of shock came from the other werewolves.

Stix glanced at them, then back to me. "Meg wants you to stay, so you'll stay. Until she lets you leave, try to keep the peace." He turned his gaze on Kiyah. "Head back home."

"But, Dad," she began.

He shook his head firmly. "Now, Kiyah."

She shot me one more glare before storming off. Stix turned away without another word and followed her.

"Good job, freak," Rhett said. "Look what you've done."

Anger filled me at everything I didn't understand and couldn't control. I rounded on him with my hands clenched into fists.

"You're the one who hit a girl," I said. "What kind of werewolf are you? Werewolves should defend their pack, not beat them into submission. I may not be an Alpha, but neither are you."

The wolf inside of me struggled to reach the surface. I wasn't sure what the rules were for being in wolf form inside the Den. No one else was. It took all of my self-control to walk away before I messed up again.

"Go ahead, cur. Walk away like the coward you are," Rhett goaded. "Prove your worthlessness and live up to expectations by running away."

Actually, it would feel great to hit someone. I spun around and clocked Rhett in the head with a haymaker. He stumbled backwards a few steps. Blood showed at the corner of his lip where my fist had connected. He put a hand to it, them brought his fingers down and looked at the blood.

A slight smile touched his lips. "That's it, freak. Maybe you've got a bit of fight in you after all!"

The spectators crowded forward into a circle. Rhett walked around me. I was careful to face him at all times. I had never actually fought before, not with fists instead of guns at least. I figured pointing that out wouldn't help me at the moment. Whenever I backed against the circle of observers, someone shoved me forward into the middle. I gritted my teeth and faced Rhett with the hope that werewolves had at least some fighting instincts that would help me.

Several punches later, I realized that wasn't the case. As hard as I tried to hit him, he slipped past my flying fists and land a punch of his own before dancing free. Only the first punch where I had caught him by surprise connected.

"What's wrong, cur?" Rhett spat. "Not only are you not an Alpha, you're not even a werewolf! Who fights like that?"

He landed yet another jab to my cheekbone. I felt it split under the blow. The sensation of blood trickling down my cheek wasn't my favorite.

"First blood!" someone called out.

"The newbie drew blood first!" a girl corrected. "He split Rhett's lip!"

"That was a surprise hit; it doesn't count," the first argued.

"Can't you hit me, freak?" Rhett teased as he dodged away from another haymaker.

If the blow had connected, the werewolf would probably be laying unconscious on the ground; unfortunately, his quick footwork and lightning-fast reflexes meant I received a punch above my ear that multiplied my headache by a hundredfold.

It was the last straw. The wolf inside me surged and I let it go. I leaped at Rhett and phased so quickly my paws slammed into his stomach before my feet had even touched the ground. He landed on his back with a shout. I lowered my muzzle and closed my fangs so that they touched the flesh of his exposed neck. He froze at the touch.

"Break it up!" a man shouted.

Out of the corner of my eye, I saw the werewolves give way again to reveal a man with dark skin and a very disapproving expression on his face. That disapproval deepened when his eyes landed on us. I backed off while keeping my gaze on Rhett in case he made any sudden moves. Fortunately for him, he appeared content to sit up slowly and watch me.

"The rules of the Den are very specific," the man who had appeared said. I caught a glimpse of the wolf head brand on his forearm that matched Meg's and the one on Stix's arm. "Phasing to wolf form during a fight not only expels one to the cage for the night, you'll get a week of rounds to cool your temper." His brow creased and he said, "Who are you? I don't recognize your wolf."

"He's the newcomer, Roundy," a girl said.

"Yeah," another echoed. "And he's cute in both forms."

They giggled.

"He attacked me," Rhett said, seeing his opening. "I almost died, Dad. He's a loose cannon."

Roundy glanced from me to the other werewolf. "Coming from you, I'd say you deserved it."

Rhett opened his mouth to argue, then shut it again and lowered his gaze sullenly.

Roundy looked back at me. "Unfortunately, newcomer or not, we have rules here that must be followed. Go phase and report to the first tunnel. You'll be spending the night in the cage. Maybe that'll warn you to take it easy around here. Peace at the Den depends on respecting those who live here." His voice gentled and he said, "You'll figure it out quickly enough.

Just give it time." He looked at the werewolves who were watching us. "The rest of you, scatter. It's bad enough that none of you thought to warn our new friend of the consequences. Egging on a fight is just as bad as participating. Stick around and you'll be spending the night in the cage with him."

They left quickly at the threat in his words, and Rhett went with them. Roundy gave me an apologetic look. "Sorry about that, but rules are rules. It's my job to see that they're obeyed. I'll give you a few minutes to collect your things." He walked away to leave me standing in the now empty teenage hangout area.

I hadn't taken the time to pull off my shirt when I phased, or unbuttoned my pants, which left them ripped and tattered from the force of changing form. Embarrassment filled me at the thought of phasing and wearing them in shame. I was really beginning to hate the Den.

"Hey."

I glanced back at the sound of Kiyah's voice. She stood in the doorway of the room with a troubled expression on her face.

She lowered her gaze at my look. "It's my fault you got in trouble." She looked back at me through her streaked hair. "To be fair, I didn't ask you to defend me." Her gaze flitted around the room in which I still stood in wolf form. "That doesn't happen here. What you said about hitting girls and all that. It's every wolf for themselves. Girls, boys, it doesn't matter. Chivalry is something I've read about in books or see in movies." She shook her head. "I never actually thought it existed in real life."

I wanted to tell her it did exist. At least in my family, my dad had always taught us to respect girls, to open the door for them, carry heavy things for them if needed, and to talk respectfully whenever one was present. But I couldn't say anything in wolf form and I sure wasn't about to phase in front of her.

I lowered my head and grabbed my torn pants in my mouth with the thought of finding somewhere to phase that would give me at least a shred of privacy.

"I know where you can get more clothes," Kiyah offered. At my look, she smiled sheepishly. "It's the least I can do for getting you into this mess."

I dropped the pants and took a step toward her. She walked past me instead and led me to the opposite side of the room.

"I've never seen anyone phase so quickly. You sure caught Rhett by surprise." She looked at me over her shoulder. "I was supposed to go home with my dad, but I gave him the slip. I had to watch what you'd do." A grin crossed her lips. "We don't have many unpredictable werewolves around here. It's discouraged because it causes disorder. You'll be lucky if rounds don't knock it out of you." Her voice lowered and she said, "But I hope not, because today was the most excitement we've had around here in months."

She pushed open a door against the far wall. A dark, bricked tunnel was revealed. Kiyah pressed a button on the wall near the door and warm lights flooded the hallway.

"We don't use the outside passages much, so they're perfect for times like these when you want to get away without a crowd watching," she said as she led the way. She glanced back at me. "And there's always a crowd watching around here. You'll be lucky to have any privacy, especially when Rhett starts telling everyone what happened. They'll all be watching." She shook her head. "It's positively annoying."

She passed several doors, then opened one that looked like all the others. The scent of laundry detergent filled my nose when I followed her inside. I wondered if that was how she knew which door she was looking for.

Two women and two men were busy pulling sheets from one of the big machines that took up an entire wall of the room.

One of the women gave me a curious look.

"Kiyah, why is your friend in wolf form?" Her gaze shifted to me. "You know it's not night yet. Meg won't be pleased."

"He, uh, lost a bet with Rhett," Kiyah quickly replied. She shot me a look. "I'm helping him save face by finding him some clothes. Can you help me, Bri? I'd really appreciate it!"

The woman looked around. "I'm sure we can scrounge up something. Restocks are a bit scarce until Meg sends out another supply run. I have a list a mile long for rounds. They'll be thrilled."

She grabbed a few items and handed them to Kiyah. "This should help." She speared with me a chiding expression. "And stay away from Rhett. He's always causing trouble." She turned away from us and shook her head as she mumbled, "That boy's gonna fail the Gauntlet if he doesn't learn to control his temper."

"Ferris made it through," the other woman pointed out.

Bri laughed. "Yeah, well, I still say it's because he had Roundy for a partner. Anyone would make it through with Roundy." Her expression sobered and she said, "And that was before the new Gauntlet. We'll be lucky if there's any kids left." She shot Kiyah an apologetic glance. "Sorry, girl."

Kiyah shrugged with a smile, but I could see the worry in her eyes when she replied, "It's no big deal. We've all got to do it, right?"

Bri nodded, but she didn't look any happier at the thought.

Kiyah pulled the door open again and motioned for me to follow her out. She gave a sigh of relief when the door shut behind us. "Thank goodness for Bri. If Kat was there, she would've reported us to my dad." She shook her head. "That last thing I need is for Dad to throw both of us in the cage."

She gave me an apologetic look. “Sorry.” She set the clothes on the ground and backed away. “Go ahead and phase. I’ll wait around the corner. Just, well, just hurry. You never know who might show up back here.”

I did as she said. It felt much better to put on the dark blue tee-shirt and basketball shorts than the clothes I had destroyed. At least I would be able to sit in whatever the cage was with some modicum of modesty.

The thought of being in a cage put me on edge. I had already been in far too many cages in my life. I hated being trapped, and I knew that wasn’t just my wolf side talking. No creature, human, monster, or animal, should be in a cage. When I was younger, I has set my kindergarten class’ pet hamsters free. The teacher had scolded me saying that the animals weren’t equipped to survive on their own. I remembered the look of horror on her face when we found a bunch of baby hamsters behind the paper cupboard a few months later.

“You ready, newbie?” Kiyah called.

“Finn,” I replied.

She poked her head around the corner. Upon seeing me clothed, she crossed toward me. “What?”

“My name,” I replied. “It’s Finn, not newbie.”

She shrugged. “Around here, you’ll be newbie until another one shows up, which is probably going to be never. Sorry about that.”

I stifled a sigh of acceptance. With any luck, I wouldn’t be around when the next werewolf showed up to take the title.

“Off to the cage?” she asked.

I nodded. “I guess so. Do you know where it is?”

“Unfortunately,” she replied. “But don’t worry. We’ve all spent our fair share of time there.”

I gave her a horrified look. “Your dad made you stay in there?”

She nodded with a sigh. "He has to be fair and all that." Her expression darkened. "Though if you ask me, stealing chocolate from Minnie isn't exactly grounds for caging, if you know what I mean."

"I don't think anything should be grounds for caging," I replied.

She had taken several steps down the hall before she gave a little exasperated sound. She spun around to face me and walked backwards to say, "You know what? You're right! Nobody should be caged. It's ridiculous and a violation of our inborn rights! Why should I be caged for stealing chocolate? Couldn't he have just told me not to take it? And as for being fair, Reba was right there with me and she didn't get punished!" She huffed. "That's what's not fair!"

I didn't realize my comment was going to open such a can of worms. I cleared my throat and said, "Maybe he thought he was teaching you a lesson?"

She was fuming when she replied, "Caging his child? He always says I have to be an example to Max and Missy, but they're six now. What's he going to do if they make a mistake?"

"Throw them in the cage?" I guessed.

She stomped a foot. "Yes, throw them in the cage." She shook her head. "It's the easy answer, I guess. We're parenting with champions here." She glanced at me. "I don't suppose you got caged when you were younger?"

I shook my head. "No. Nobody gets caged where I'm from unless they do something really bad and get thrown in jail. But that's for people who threaten lives, murdering and stealing and all that." I paused and quickly corrected, "Not exactly like stealing chocolate, unless you get caught shoplifting. You might go to juvie for that."

"What's juvie?" she asked.

"It's another kind of cage," I replied.

She nodded as if that made perfect sense. We continued on in silence until she looked back at me. "I'm still sorry you have to spend your first night in the cage. It doesn't seem fair."

I forced a nonchalant smile and said, "I'll be fine."

Her eyes narrowed as she watched me. It made me uncomfortable. "What?" I asked.

Red brushed her cheeks and she turned away. "Nothing."

I refused to let it drop. "What is it?"

She glanced back at me, then ducked her head again to hide behind her silver and pink hair. "I was just, uh, wondering if all the boys outside the Den are as handsome as you."

I felt heat rise with my own embarrassment and looked away before she could see how her words affected me. "There's all types out there," I said blandly.

She turned a corner and began to whistle. It made me smile to see her uncomfortable as well.

"Can I ask you a question?" I dared to ask.

She stopped whistling. "Sure."

"Do you think you could show me where they're keeping my friend? I just want to check on him before I'm locked up in a cage all night."

She considered my request for a moment. "That sounds fair. But if we're caught, I'll be thrown in the cage, too."

"We won't get caught," I reassured her. "I just need to know he's alright."

"I guess that can't harm anything," she said. "It's not far."

Chapter Three

KIYAH SLOWED BEFORE WE reached the tunnel she was looking for. We listened for any sign that others were around. It was strange to see someone else use their ears and nose the same way I was learning to. It made me feel less alone in a strange, almost desperate way I kept to myself.

Kiyah led me to the end of the tunnel. I could smell Vicken's earthy, blood-tinged scent and my heart sped up. Kiyah pushed open the door a crack, peeked inside, then opened it wider. The smell of blood flooded out.

"Vicken?" I said as soon as I entered the room.

The sight of his pale, still form chained to a circular platform at the far end of the room made my blood run cold. I ran to the platform and dropped to my knees.

"Vicken, wake up," I pleaded.

His head turned with my shaking and my breath caught in my throat. Dark blood coated the side of his face.

"What happened?" I whispered in shock.

I touched the blood and pulled my fingers back to check. The fluid was too dark. A puddle beneath his head showed that nobody had tried to stop the bleeding. Head wounds always bled more than other wounds and he had definitely lost too much.

"Vicken, you stay with me," I said, forcing my voice to remain steady.

"I don't know what happened to him," Kiyah said.

I ignored her and yanked my tee-shirt off. I tore it into long strips.

"Easy," I whispered, hoping he could hear me.

I wrapped the strips around his head to keep pressure against the wound. I didn't know if he even had enough blood left to bleed anymore. The thought made my heart tighten in fear.

"He needs blood," I said to Kiyah. I brought my wrist to my mouth.

"What are you doing in here?" an angry voice demanded.

I looked back to see Stix storm into the room with four other werewolves.

"He just wanted to check on his friend before he went into the cage," Kiyah replied quickly.

Stix's gaze darkened. "Kiyah, you're supposed to be at home."

"I know, Dad," she began.

Stix cut her off. "Leave us." When she didn't move, he barked, "Now!"

Kiyah threw me an apologetic look before she ran from the room.

"Just let me give him some blood," I told the advancing werewolves.

"You were supposed to be in the cage ten minutes ago," Stix said. "I didn't think I'd have to track you down."

"They hurt my friend," I replied. "Somebody needs to help him!"

Stix glanced at the vampire. His lips twisted in disgust before he looked at one of the other werewolves. "What happened?"

"He woke up," the werewolf said. "He tried to attack us. We had to shoot him." His eyes lowered. "But the bullet hit him in the head."

Stix glared at him. "You know the danger of shooting someone so close. This is your mess. Clean it up."

Stix grabbed my arm.

I broke free of his grasp. "Just let me give him some blood," I said. "I'll go with you. But let me help him first."

Stix shook his head. "You have an obligation." He removed the thick handcuffs from where they had been hanging on his belt. "Either you go willingly or we drag you there." His eyes narrowed. "I'd recommend the former."

My teeth bared in a snarl. "Let. Me. Help. My. Friend." I spaced the words carefully, my rage barely under control.

"Your friend may survive your stupidity," Stix replied. "But you won't if you don't come with us of your own free will."

Another werewolf tried to grab me. I jumped over Vicken and brought my wrist to my mouth. "Give me a chance," I pleaded.

"You don't have any more chances," Stix growled.

His gun was in his hand at the blink of an eye. The thought that Vicken would die if I didn't help him fueled my recklessness. I threw myself into Stix, bowling him over and catching up the gun. I rolled up to my knees and shot the four other werewolves in quick succession. I was about to turn my gun on Stix when something slammed into the side of my head. I fell to the ground and heard Stix open the manacles he had used to clobber me.

"I told Meg he'd be a loose cannon," the werewolf muttered as my arms were pulled roughly behind my back.

My head lolled forward when they picked me up by the handcuffs and my ankles and carried me from the room.

"What about the vampire?" a werewolf asked.

"Leave him," Stix replied. "This one just sealed his friend's fate."

Panic flooded through me. I tried to fight, but my limbs wouldn't respond. I willed the wolf to come to the forefront, but the blow to the head had dazed my ability to phase. I lost track of the twists and turns down various hallways until a door swung open with a creak and I was tossed inside. Hitting the floor filled me with enough adrenaline that I was able to lumber to my feet and throw myself against the barred door.

Stix backed away with the key in his hand and a look of relief on his face that he had locked the door in time.

"Let me out!" I yelled.

"There's no way," Stix replied. "You're in here for your own good."

I hit the door again without regard for how pain flooded my shoulder at the blow.

"Open this door!" I demanded.

Stix took a step forward. I was aware of other werewolves watching us from further away. Apparently seeing someone be thrown in the cage was a community event. I doubted they had ever been so entertained.

"You better watch yourself," Stix growled low enough that his voice was pitched only for me. "You're playing a very dangerous game here."

I willed my voice to match his; it was difficult with the way my heart hammered in my chest and the ringing echoed loudly in my ears from being hit in the head. "Just please, let me out. I need to take care of my friend. I'll do it. You don't have to worry about him. Just let me do it. That's all I ask." Tears burned in my eyes at the thought of the state in which I had found Vicken.

Stix shook his head. "I can't let you out."

I leaned against the bars, my voice pleading, "Then please, please promise me you'll give him some blood. Please. I'll do anything. I'll be the perfect example. I'll stay here as long as you want me to. Just please save my friend." The tears fell down my cheeks.

Stix let out a breath. "I can't do that. I'm sorry." He turned and motioned for the other werewolves to leave.

"Please?" I called out, my voice as broken as my heart.

Stix walked away as though he didn't hear me. Sobs tore from my chest. I raged against the bars with my hands cuffed behind my back until I fell to my knees, exhausted. Sometime during my battle with the door, even the last of the spectating werewolves had wandered away. Apparently the pain of the new werewolf didn't affect them.

I fell exhausted to my side with my back against the door. The thought of Vicken chained and dying made me want to curl up in the fetal position and shut out the world, but even that had been denied to me with the way my wrists were locked. I fell into a numb state of staring at the inside of the cage without really seeing it, my thoughts on my dying friend and my head in constant pain.

I had no idea how much time had passed before I heard the sound of a sneaker on the marble floor.

"Finn?"

I couldn't bring myself to move.

I heard the faint sound of fabric on metal, and then a hand touched my arm. The smell of blood made me glance down even through the numb haze of my mind. The hand was small and the fingernails painted pink and black, but what drew my eyes was the cloth wrapped around the wrist. I stared at it.

Another manicured hand with matching fingernails slipped through the bars and unwrapped the cloth. It fell away to reveal a shallow cut with a deep hole on either side.

"But," I began, willing my brain to work. "What, I mean, why? I mean, what did you—"

"You were much better at talking earlier," Kiyah said. "I know my dad hits hard, but this is ridiculous."

I struggled to a sitting position and turned to face her.

Kiyah's expression fell. "He hit you really hard."

I couldn't feel anything past amazement at what she had shown me. "Vicken. Did you? I mean is he? I mean, did you let him drink?"

Kiyah nodded. "Yeah, I did. It took some urging, but I finally got him to take a few gulps."

I could see in her light blue eyes how bad he was. I didn't want to ask, but made myself say in a whisper, "Is he going to be alright?"

Kiyah's eyebrows pulled together. She pushed a strand of pink hair from her face and said, "I'm not going to lie. He's not in a good place, but I'll make sure he eats and I'll keep an eye on him for you."

The relief that someone in this horrid place had at least some shred of humanity made my heart hurt. I leaned my forehead against the bars and let out a half-sigh, half-sob at the thought that Vicken wasn't dead, that there was hope, and that someone in the Den wasn't afraid of him.

Kiyah's hand touched my head. "Are you okay, Finn?"

I sat back on my heels and nodded. "I am now." I took a steadying breath. "Thank you. I don't know how I'll ever repay you, but I will. I promise."

Kiyah's gaze held mine. "You'll get me out of here."

My eyes widened. "What?"

Kiyah leaned closer to the bars. "If you and the vampire get out, you take me with you. I can't stay in this place any longer. It's killing me."

"Vicken," I told her.

"What?" she asked, caught off-guard.

"The vampire's name is Vicken. Vicken Ruvine the Third." I held her gaze. "And if you keep him alive until I can get us out of here, I promise to take you with us."

Kiyah was silent for a moment before she nodded. "Good. I'll take care of him. You take care of yourself. You're in a lot of trouble."

I sighed and leaned my back against the bars. "Tell me something I don't know."

"You don't know the rules around here," Kiyah replied from behind me. "Like, if you hurt someone inside the Den, you have to answer for it in your hide."

I glanced back at her in confusion. "In my hide? Like a whipping?"

She nodded. "And after that, Meg's going to make you run in the Gauntlet. I overheard her say it's the only way to prove whether you're fit to be here."

I turned away from Kiyah. "I don't care if I'm fit to be here. I don't want to be here. They're the ones forcing me."

"Yeah, but if you don't run in the Gauntlet or you don't pass, they'll kill you."

A chill ran through my body at her words. I turned slowly on my knees to face her. "They'll kill me?"

She lowered her gaze. "It's how they weed out the weak. Meg says we can't have werewolves running all over without order, so they use the trials to figure out who is a valuable asset to the Pack. Anyone who passes is given the Den brand on their forearm. The rest are thrown to the bears."

I tried to understand what she was telling me. I didn't know if it was the blow to the head or the relief of knowing that

Vicken was alive, but her words didn't make sense. I shook my head. "That's ridiculous. They throw werewolves who don't pass the Gauntlet to bears? What happens then?"

"They're eaten," she said with a tone that hinted at the stupidity of my question.

I watched her closely. "So let me get this straight. I'm going to be whipped and then thrown into some sort of trial, and if I fail, I get thrown to bears to be eaten. But if I survive, I get to stay in this glorious place as a member of the Pack?"

The wryness of my tone wasn't lost on her. She gave a half-smile and said, "Maybe you're better off dead."

"I'm beginning to think that," I replied.

Kiyah glanced behind her. "I've got to get back before Dad finds out I'm gone. I'll have Bri sneak you some food if she gets a chance. You need to focus on what's ahead." Worry showed in her blue gaze when she said, "The Gauntlet is hard, Finn, and the new one is even harder. A lot of good werewolves aren't going to survive." The pain that swept across her face told of loved ones she had lost.

"Does everyone do the Gauntlet?" I asked.

She nodded. "We usually do it when we turn eighteen, but Meg said with your tendencies, she would waive the age restriction for the good of the Pack."

"Sixteen isn't that far off," I replied.

She sighed. "Tell me about it. We practice from the time we can walk. More than half of the werewolves who go through the Gauntlet don't make it."

My mouth fell open. "You mean more than half of the werewolves here are thrown to the bears before they're adults?"

She nodded. "Those who don't die in the Gauntlet, and we've been training for it our whole lives. You're going to be at a heavy disadvantage. Just remember to keep your head and obey the rules. They'll throw you to the bears if you slip up."

Her gaze darkened. "They keep the bears hungry so they stay angry. The last time I told Dad that treating animals that way made us less than the animals, I got slapped." She gritted her teeth and said, "Get me out of here, Finn."

I nodded. "I will. Just keep my friend alive."

"I will," she replied.

Footsteps sounded down the hall. Kiyah ghosted away without a backwards glance. I moved back from the door, but kept my gaze on it. I didn't mind that Kiyah had touched my arm through the bars, but nobody else was going to get that close.

My reservations strengthened when Meg, Stix, Roundy, and a skinny werewolf who was missing a hand appeared.

I rose to my feet despite the way my head pounded. I might not have had much dignity left with handcuffs and standing behind bars, but I refused to put up a weak front. I watched them approach the cage.

Meg sighed when she reached the door. "You've managed to stir up a whole lot of trouble in a very short amount of time."

I glared at her. "You promised my friend would be safe. You lied."

She glanced at Stix. "What's he talking about?"

Stix cleared his throat with an uncomfortable expression. "Mancos accidentally shot the vamp in the head. Apparently, the vampire woke up and tried to attack them." At Meg's searching look, he admitted, "The vampire's not doing so good."

"He was bleeding out," I told Meg hotly. "They left him there to die." I crossed to the bars and felt a brief satisfaction when everyone but Meg stepped back. "You promised he'd be safe, and they left him to die. That's why I attacked them. I was trying to save my friend's life. As a werewolf, you should understand that."

Meg watched me in silence for a moment before she turned her glare on Stix. "If that vampire dies, it's on your head."

"But, Meg—" he began.

She cut him off. "A promise has been made, Stix. I put you in charge of the vampire's wellbeing and promised Finn he would be safe. The failure is on your shoulders." Her voice lowered threateningly when she said, "If he dies while in the Den, you will be thrown to the bears."

Stix's mouth fell open. "But-but my children!"

Meg lifted a shoulder. "You made your bed, Stix. You better hope the vampire doesn't die."

Stix threw me a glare before he stormed back up the hallway.

"Thank you," I started to say, but Meg cut me off.

"As for you, order is very important in keeping this place safe. And you've thrown order to the wind. The last thing we need is some sort of rebel telling our children that there's a better life out there for them." She toyed with something in her hand. It took me a moment to realize it was a whip with frayed ends. "You hurt members of my pack, Finn. You're right when you say that I would fight to protect any of my family's lives. I may not understand why you call a vampire your friend, but the same rules apply. Hurt for hurt; pain for pain." She let the end of the whip fall to the ground. A twitch of her wrist made it move like a snake along the floor. "Tonight, you'll pay for attacking members of the Pack. Tomorrow, you'll be thrown in the Gauntlet. If you survive, you can stay. If not, well, the bears are hungry."

Her gaze held mine with a glimmer of threat. I returned her stare with a threat of my own. "You don't scare me, Meg." I tipped my head to indicate the main area of the Den visible beyond the far wall of my cage. Werewolves had gathered there without me noticing. At least half of those watching were close to my age. I felt Vicken's haughtiness on my face when I said to Meg, "You're the one running some sick game here, controlling the youth with your rules and threats. They deserve freedom. They deserve to see what lies beyond these walls. Instead, they grow up with the fear that they're going to die from whatever is in the Gauntlet before they've even had a chance to live! What kind of childhood is that?"

I lowered my voice but kept it pitched for the others to hear. "You're the reason there aren't any werewolves beyond these walls, but you can't keep them in here forever. You can't shield them from a world that isn't nearly as bad as you've made it out to be." I read the truth of my words on her face and continued with, "You might have made up for the lack of Alphas by death threats and false promises of safety, but the world is waiting out there and the youth in here should have a chance to experience it. You can't block it out forever; all you can do is raise your pack in a way that they're prepared to face it." Murmurs rose from the werewolves on the other side of my cage. I couldn't tell if they agreed or not.

I stepped back from the door. "I'll take your punishment and I'll face the Gauntlet. But if I survive, I'm leaving the Den and I'm taking Vicken with me." I turned and faced the youth directly. "And any of you who want to get out and see what this world is all about can join me." I heard the cage door open behind me, but ignored the werewolves' advance. "There's safety at the Academy and enough room for all of you." Hands grabbed my arms. I moved my eyes from one teenager to another. Those who met my gaze did so eagerly. "And if I don't make it out, tell them Finn sent you. They'll let you in. I promise."

"Stop talking," Meg growled in my ear.

I fought back a grim smile at the suppressed panic in her voice and continued with, "There is life beyond these walls. Don't let your elders hold you back. Choose to live your own life, not one that's been dictated for you. Choose—"

A stunner bullet struck me in the back. I dropped to my knees and was pulled out of the cage, but not before I saw the light and excitement on the faces of the teenagers who had listened to me.

Satisfaction bloomed in my chest even as I was strapped to a whipping post in the middle of the compound. I didn't struggle. Meg expected me to, as apparent by the number of armed guards that kept the audience at a distance who had gathered to watch my punishment. By the looks of things, she had required every werewolf in the Den to be a spectator. The sight of babies in arms and toddlers holding the cloth of their mother's dresses in chubby fingers made me sick.

Kiyah's voice saying, 'We practice from the time we can walk,' repeated over again in my head. Meg had a good hold on her pack. She trained them from birth to fear her command. It was a twisted but effective way to keep her control over them. I vowed to break that hold if there was any way to do so.

"Join with me, brothers and sisters, in reciting the pledge of the Den," Meg instructed.

On cue, the rest of the werewolves called out with her, "Strength of one, strength of the Pack, life for one, life for the Pack. We unite in safety, progress, and prosperity. In every action, we work for the good of the Pack; in every deed, we strive for peace. Hierarchy is safety, and the rules will be obeyed. Strength of one, strength of the Pack."

From my viewpoint strapped to the crossbeam of the post and with my head facing down, I saw Meg nod out of the corner of my eye.

"Very good. As you know, Finn is a stranger to our rules, but he has broken them, nonetheless." She turned. "Roundy, recite the rules this werewolf has broken."

Roundy lifted his deep voice. "One count of insubordination. Two counts of threatening a Pack member, six counts of injury to other members of the Pack, and one count of phasing to attack a Pack member."

Murmurs ran through the crowd. I guessed they thought throwing in the werewolves that I had shot at the accident would help give fuel to the fire against me. I would have smiled if my face wasn't still frozen under the effects of the numbing electricity.

Meg took over. "Per Den guidelines, Finn is to be punished with one lash per injured pack member."

The murmurs increased.

"Finn will also be required to run the Gauntlet and prove that he is an asset to our pack instead of a threat," Meg concluded.

The talking rose to a roar of surprised voices.

"But he's too young," one woman pointed out. "Children should be eighteen to attempt the Gauntlet."

"He's already proven to be a threat," I heard Rhett say. "Throw him to the bears!"

A man yelled, "That's too many lashes for a boy."

"He has to pay the price," another said.

"That's not fair," a girl called out. I recognized Kiyah's voice. As much as I appreciated her standing up for me, I didn't want to cause further trouble for her at the Den.

"Quiet," Stix growled.

"It has been decided," Meg said firmly. "Roundy, you can begin."

The first lash sliced across my back with a sharp hiss. I heard a few whispers from members of the crowd, but everyone else watched in silence. By the second and third lashes, comments of, "He's not making a sound," and "It's unnatural," could be heard. But Meg had done me a favor when she shot me. I was sure she had no idea how much the stunner bullet had numbed my entire body. I could feel the impact of the lash, but the sting of the slice across my skin and the feeling of blood down my back was lost.

"Maybe he is an Alpha," I heard one man say when Roundy lashed me for the last time.

I saw a few drops of blood fall from the whip when the werewolf wound it up before handing it to Meg.

"Carry him back to the cage," Meg ordered, her voice level. She bent down and whispered for only me to hear, "You have one night to heal, then it's onto the Gauntlet. You sealed your own fate this time, Finn."

She rose and lifted her voice to say, "The rules have spoken. We will see you all in the spectators' room tomorrow."

The chains on the crossbeam were unwound. As I was dragged from the stocks, my last glimpse was of Kiyah's wide eyes. She held up her hand to show me the colored handkerchief she had wrapped around her wrist. At least Vicken would be cared for.

Chapter Four

I MADE A SHOW of not being stiff the next morning when I was escorted to a moving truck and loaded inside. Werewolves had turned out to see me go. I didn't know whether to feel touched by their efforts or worried. Several of the teenagers wore handkerchiefs like Kiyah's around their wrists. When I walked past, they lifted them to ensure that I noticed.

"Represent," one boy said quietly.

"Alpha strong," another called out.

A skinny girl of no more than twelve held out her thin wrist and said, "I'll be cheering for you."

The adults, their wolf brands visible on their forearms, didn't look pleased at what their children were doing.

"Good riddance," an older woman with gray streaks in her hair said.

A man with a bushy beard leaned against the truck as I was shoved inside and said, "I hope you rot out there, boy."

The door was pulled shut and I listened to a lock close. There weren't any seats in the back of the moving truck. In order to keep from falling over with the swaying after each bump, I sat down near the back door and leaned against the wall. My breath caught and I tipped forward again.

Despite the long night of moonlight that fell handily along one side of the cage, my back had only partially healed. I figured that the same bullet that had done me the favor of numbing my skin during the lashing had also impeded the healing process. Out of the clothing brought to me the next morning, I had chosen a black shirt to wear so that it could hide any blood from the whip marks. The last thing I wanted to do was show weakness around the other werewolves.

The sound of the truck's tires changed from pavement to dirt. It bumped and jolted along a dirt road for at least twenty minutes before it stopped. Relief that we were no longer moving was chased away by the sound of footsteps and the reminder of what was to come.

"Up and out, boy," Roundy said when he pushed up the sliding door.

A glanced to my right showed Rhett, two other boys, and a girl with long red hair waiting in front of a posh SUV. I had apparently been deemed not fit to ride with these other potential candidates for the Pack. I tried to find an inkling of feeling at the slight, but there wasn't any. I wanted to be far away from any member of the Den, be they a potential Pack member or not.

"Now that we're all present," Roundy said with a glare at me as though I was to blame for the delay, "We can begin." He waved a hand around in a bored gesture as though he had said the same words many times. "As you can see, the entire Gauntlet is monitored by cameras. Most of you have family who will be cheering you on from the spectators' room. Even though you can't hear them, know that they are pulling for you to succeed."

His gaze was on his son. Rhett appeared nervous and excited at the same time. He grinned at me, showing the gap in his teeth. "Unless you're Finn. He's all alone."

Roundy barely spared me a glance before he continued with, "You are the first group to attempt the new and improved Gauntlet. You have trained for this since you could walk; now is your chance to show us that you belong to the Pack." His pride was evident in the way he looked the other teenagers over. "You can complete each of the three trials in wolf or human form. The choice is entirely yours. But you must complete each leg of the Gauntlet by yourself. No assistance is allowed." He gave his son and the other three werewolves a big smile. "Good luck, do your best, and we'll be cheering for you to reach the end and become an official member of the Pack." He held out his arm to show the wolf head brand. "Make us proud, children. You can do this."

At his motion, we headed toward a ladder that peeked out from the top of what appeared to be a deep canyon. I glanced back to see Roundy grab Rhett in a tight hug. He then held his son out at arm's length.

"Make us proud, son," he said, his eyes bright.

"I will," Rhett replied.

He caught me watching and glared. I turned away and followed the others to the edge of the canyon. The ladder led straight down the side. A glance along it showed that the steps of the ladder ended about four rungs down and it was made up of merely two poles from there to the bottom. The side of the rock wall dipped inward so that the ladder was suspended in the air for the final thirty feet.

"Down to go up," the girl said.

"Right," the taller of the two other the boys confirmed. "Just like we trained. Remember, Lunera, keep a loose grip and let your body weight pull you down."

"I've got it, Ross," Lunera replied in an annoyed tone. "Just don't come clobbering down on top of me."

She stepped around the ladder and then looked at Rhett. For the first time, I saw a hint of uncertainty in her gaze.

Rhett gave an encouraging nod. "You've got this."

Lunera let out a breath, then moved her legs to the outside of the ladder and slid down.

I stared after her, watching in amazement until she hit the ground, then waved up at us.

"Come on, boys! That's how it's done!" she shouted.

"That's right, cur," Ross said with a laugh. "You're going to have to keep up. Too bad your Alphaness won't help you here."

"Good one," the shorter boy replied. He shoved Ross' shoulder and nearly sent him over the edge of the canyon.

"Watch it, Durnin," Ross snapped.

"Sorry," Durnin immediately apologized.

Rhett ignored them and stepped around the ladder. He slid down even faster than Lunera had done.

"I'm going before you push me over," Ross growled with a glare at the other boy.

"At least you'd get to the bottom quickly," Durnin replied sullenly as his friend slid down. He followed without a glance in my direction.

I sucked in a steeling breath and then swung around the side of the ladder. I didn't have to wonder if my movements appeared fumbling compared to the others. The thought of merely holding on with the insides of my ankles and a grip on the poles made my heart pound in my chest. A quick look around showed that there was no other way down. It was either slide or become bear fodder.

I gritted my teeth and slipped my ankles around the outside of the poles. Loosening my grip was harder than I thought. Apparently, the wolf side of me thought sliding down was hazardous to my health. I couldn't have agreed more.

My heart leaped into my throat when I opened my hands slightly and slid about ten feet. I accidentally grabbed the left pole harder than the right. I jerked to the left, my feet slipped clear of the poles, and I hung suspended with only the grip of my left hand keeping me from plummeting to the bottom of the canyon. It took a few heart-pounding seconds to swing back and get my feet and both of my hands situated again. The healing burn from the demon fire on my right palm made the skin a bit more slippery than the left. Keeping that in mind, I gripped hard and waited to catch my breath.

"Look at the wimp," Rhett called up. "You going to hang around up there all day?" He laughed, then said, "Come on, guys. He's not going to make it."

Fueled by the boy's words, I opened my hands again. The rock wall sped by so fast the details blurred. I hit the ground with a thump that made dust rise from beneath my shoes. I turned to find the other werewolves watching me. By the looks on their faces, I had apparently done something right.

I cleared my throat. "So, was that the first leg of the Gauntlet?"

Lunera grinned and turned away. Rhett rolled his eyes. "I thought you were stupid before. Thanks for confirming it."

Durnin and Ross laughed and followed Rhett. I guessed doing one thing right didn't account for much in the Gauntlet.

Determined not to ask any more stupid questions, I trailed behind the others. It wasn't many steps before I caught up to where they were staring up the wall on the other side of the canyon.

"Up and over," Lunera said.

"You've got to be kidding me," I muttered.

Rhett threw me a challenging look. "What's wrong, cur? Afraid of a little climb?"

I didn't reply. Lunera started up. She made it look easy, placing each hand and foot methodically to climb up what looked like the nearly sheer face of the wall. Rhett moved further down, then started up his own path.

"This is my least favorite part," Ross grumbled. "Tall people weren't made to climb."

"Stop complaining," Durnin said. "You try scaling a wall with my arms and legs. At least you have a decent wingspan."

I moved away from the pair and began to climb a few feet from Rhett. I had never actually tried to scale the side of a cliff before. I figured if I got stuck, I could keep an eye on how Rhett was doing it and move over to follow him.

It was slow going. The sun was beating on our backs by the time we neared the top. Sweat trickled down my shoulder blades and stung the lash marks across my back. My throat was dry and my forearms ached from carrying my weight by my fingertips. I took my time, breathing in through my nose and out through my mouth to make sure I didn't get winded. Luckily, the others didn't seem in a hurry, either. Each of us concentrated on clearing the top and gaining a much-needed rest. We were almost there. I just needed to take my time.

A shout made my fingers slip from their handhold. Fortunately, my other hand and my feet were secure. I looked up to see Lunera slide past Rhett and then tumble from the wall. Everyone watched, shocked, as she hit the wall once about halfway down before she landed with a thump at the bottom. Any hope I had that she might survive the fall vanished at the sight of her broken body and her head twisted at an unnatural angle. Red spilled out to cover the dirt around her.

Rhett swore above me. I thought about the way Lunera had fallen, sliding past him before she plummeted to the ground below. He could have caught her. It may have pulled him from the wall or threatened his progress, but for a moment, he'd had the chance to save her life.

I saw the same realization on Rhett's face. Horror warred with guilt in his eyes as he stared down at her body. His gaze shifted from the girl to me. The emotions were replaced by a wall of anger.

"Too bad that's not you down there, cur," Rhett growled.

"Yeah, cur," Durnin said in a shaky voice. "You should join Lunera."

The sound of her name had a sobering effect on the group. Rhett grunted, then continued his climb upward. Ross and Durnin followed. I couldn't help picturing Lunera's family in the spectator room at the Den as they watched their daughter plummet to the ground. Perhaps the Pack considered her too weak to join them, maybe she didn't have what it took to survive at the Den, but she didn't have to die. She would have been welcome at the Academy. Of that, I was certain. I gritted my teeth and climbed upward with the vow that I would help any other child of the Den find safety before falling to such a meaningless death.

I pulled myself over the lip of the cliff in time to see the others enter a large tunnel. We were about two-thirds of the way up the canyon. The lip I rolled onto had been dug about twenty feet into the wall of the canyon. The tunnel the others walked into snaked into the wall at an angle. The ceiling, sides, and ground were cement. I could only imagine how long it had taken to build.

"Divide and conquer," Ross said from inside.

My ears were met by a high-pitched humming sound when I ducked into the darkness. It took a moment for my eyes to adjust to the grays of the wolf. When they did, I wanted to leave the tunnel again.

The tunnel split into five branches that ran side-by-side. Within each branch, I could see the source of the sound. Saws of every shape and size littered the small tunnels. Some were as tall as me while others were no bigger than my hand. These popped up at random places from the floor and swung from the ceiling. It looked as though we had stepped into a house of horrors where the horror was getting chopped into little pieces.

"Is this some kind of sick joke?" I asked.

All three boys looked back at me.

"Does it look like a joke?" Rhett shot back levelly.

I nodded. "Actually, it does." I gestured toward the saws and then at the cameras suspended every few feet down the tunnel. "It looks as though this pack you're so eager to join is just as eagerly awaiting the chance to see you get shredded to pieces. Is this really how they expect their sons and daughters to prove their worth?" I shook my head. "If that's what it means to be in a pack, I'm glad I don't have one. You guys need to seriously rethink your allegiance here."

Durnin looked at the saws and then back at me. "But we don't have a choice." The whining in his voice carried a heavy dose of fear.

"Yeah," Ross agreed. He glanced at one of the cameras as if worried about being overheard. "If we don't go, we'll get fed to the bears."

"Can I just point out that even the cruelest creatures in this world don't feed their young to others?" I replied.

The two boys looked from me to Rhett.

"What do we do?" Ross asked, his voice quiet.

Rhett glared at me. "We make it through the tunnel and face the last leg of the Gauntlet. It's what you've trained for." He crossed his arms as he glared at his friends. "Ross, do you really want to disappoint your grandma? And Durnin, you take first every year in the obstacle courses."

"Yeah, but they weren't trying to kill me," Durnin replied with his gaze on the cement floor at his feet.

Rhett sighed and spoke so that his voice was just audible above the hum of the saws. "I know it looks scary, but you've trained for this. You can do it, both of you. We're going to come out of the Gauntlet and get our brands together. Who's with me?" He held out his hand.

Ross immediately put his on top. Durnin hesitated, glanced at me, and then put his hand on the others.

"I can't let my family down," the werewolf said by way of apology.

"They let you down by expecting you to do this," I replied, eyeing the saws. "Death by bears sounds pretty inviting right now."

"Wolf up, freak," Rhett growled. He looked at his friends. "I'm doing this in wolf form. There's not much clearance in there. You'll be more agile."

He pulled his shirt off, followed by his shoes and shorts. The others turned away and did the same. Out of the corner of my eye, I saw Rhett fold his shorts into a tight bundle and then wrap the drawstring around it. He tied a loop in the end before he phased.

Grateful for the shorts Kiyah had given me, I quickly did the same. I phased and was in wolf form in time to see all three boys duck their heads and ease the cord of their shorts over their snouts and one paw. Using a series of practiced motions, their bundled shorts soon rested across their shoulder blades.

It took me far longer to figure out how to make it happen, but after several ungraceful, ridiculous movements that no doubt caused plenty of hilarity to the spectators at the Den, my shorts rested between my shoulders where they wouldn't impede my movements.

I looked up to see that the others had already started their journey inside the tunnels. Each had chosen a different one. I figured that was part of the rules. Grumbling inwardly to myself about the idiocy of blind followers, I picked one of the two remaining tunnels. The thought that Lunera would have taken the last one if she had survived reminded me how serious my situation was.

The saws were no joke. I ducked one that swung above my head, sidestepped another that would have sliced through my paws, and narrowly missed the next one that shot from one side of the tunnel to the other suspended on some sort of metal line. My heart raced and I could barely catch my breath. I felt as if I was on the edge of dying. The realization of my impending doom ran through my head.

I was about to jump over another saw when a thought struck me. I had done this before.

It wasn't real, of course. I would definitely have remembered my life hanging by a thread as I maneuvered around a metal-toothed obstacle course. I may not have lived it, but I had played a game similar to it.

Drake and I used to play video games together after school if we weren't hanging out with friends. One of his favorites involved getting a character from the beginning of a deadly maze to the exit. One of the segments looked pretty much like the challenge I faced. Drake used to run his character through in a mad dash, dodging, jumping, and rolling whenever he could to avoid the saws, bombs, and lasers, but his method inevitably resulted in the character's demise. I, on the other hand, had found it best to take it slow and figure out the patterns of the objects trying to kill me. Once I knew where they were predetermined to hit, I could easily make my way to the other side. It drove Drake crazy and made me the winner enough times that we eventually quit the game.

A scream sounded. My heart clenched at the thought of what one of the other boys was experiencing. I gritted my teeth and willed my mind to accept my route instead of Drake's. The wolf side of me that demanded I escape such a dangerous place acceded to the reasoning of my human side. I pulled my tail between my legs so it wouldn't get cut off and counted the seconds between the next saw's movements.

Two seconds, a slash, then the saw after it shot up from the ground to about stomach height before it disappeared back into the cement. After it, a swinging saw sliced through the air low enough to sever my spinal cord. I counted to three, watched two saws jut in from either side of the tunnel, then a third one bigger than me rose from the ground and cut through the tunnel completely. It spun for four seconds before it lowered slowly back down.

A grim grin that probably appeared like a snarl to the spectators crossed my face. I had this.

Each second matched the beat of my heart as I twisted and dove, ran, then paused before throwing myself into the next available watching position. No matter how many times I wanted to dart forward, I made myself wait for the count. The fresh air at the end of the tunnel drew closer. I didn't allow it to make me careless. Instead, I counted to ten the way Julianne had taught me and willed my thoughts to remain calm. Within each beat, I memorized the motions of the blades. They lost their power as life-ending instruments able to cause pain and death; instead, I saw only objects to be dodged, game pieces to be avoided. In the back of my mind, I pretended I battled Drake for a chance to win the game. The thought kept me calm with its familiarity, and I found myself at the other end of the tunnel before I even realized it.

"I lost a finger," Ross was in the middle of complaining when I emerged.

Ross and Rhett both shot me surprised glances.

"You're harder to kill than you look," Rhett said. His expression left little doubt how he felt about it.

I phased in the corner and pulled on my shorts. When I turned back around, I caught him staring at my back that had begun to bleed again as a result of the phase.

"What?" I snapped. "Happy to see me bleed?"

Rhett appeared momentarily ashamed. He shook his head as he turned away. "I didn't know you weren't healed from the lashing."

I crossed my arms in front of my bare chest. "It doesn't make a difference here."

"Yeah," Ross said as he wrapped a piece of cloth he had torn from his shorts around his hand to stop the bleeding from his missing index finger. "At least the blood means he's not some kind of demon."

"Demons bleed," I replied quietly. I kept my gaze on Durnin's tunnel. "Any sign of him?"

Rhett shook his head. The thick scent of blood from the tunnel was impossible to miss.

"I heard a scream," Ross said.

Rhett nodded. "I did, too. I just hoped it wasn't bad, but he's not here." His voice was gruff to hide how he felt about it. He turned away. "Come on. We're almost done." The cold detachment in his voice didn't fool me. He couldn't hide his sorrow at the loss of his friends, but he knew he had to keep going. I found myself respecting his strength even though I couldn't understand the way he blindly followed Meg's command.

Ross and I followed the werewolf out of the tunnel. The setting sun lit another branch of the canyon in golden light below us. Five ropes hung suspended from stakes in the ground.

"So we climb down and that's it?" I asked hopefully.

Rhett glanced at me. "You can tell yourself that."

"What?" I asked. I looked from him to Ross. "Tell me what I'm missing."

Ross pointed without a word toward the other end of the canyon fork. I followed his finger to a huge cement barrier across the entire canyon.

"We climb another wall?" I guessed.

Rhett shook his head. "We survive." He grabbed one of the ropes and walked toward the edge.

"We've done enough surviving," I said. "This is stupid."

When Ross ignored me and joined Rhett at the edge, I finally snapped. I grabbed Rhett's throat and lifted him up so that we were eye to eye with his feet dangling over the edge of the canyon.

Surprise by my strength and his precarious situation showed on the eighteen-year-old's face.

"What do we survive?" I growled.

"Th-that," Rhett said, his voice tight past my grip. "Ross sh-showed you. Th-the dam."

I took a step back so Rhett's feet could touch the ground, but kept my grip on the taller boy's throat. I looked at the wall and then back at him. "That's a dam?"

Rhett nodded. "It's holding the water back."

"And then?" I prompted.

"When we reach the bottom of the canyon, they send the water down," Ross said from where he waited at the edge.

Chapter Five

I LET RHETT GO. He hunched over with his hands on his knees and drew in a breath. The realization of what he was implying sunk in. My hands clenched into fists as I stared at the canyon.

"So we survive a flood," I said. "That's just great. And these are normal situations for werewolves?" I looked at Rhett and then Ross. "It doesn't bother you that you have to survive these extremely unnatural scenarios in order to become a member of your pack? You know this is ridiculous!"

Rhett glanced at Ross, then met my gaze. "It may be ridiculous," he began. His eyes found one of the cameras on a pole above us. He looked back at me and said, "But you don't understand. There's nowhere else to go. If we don't pass the Gauntlet, we gladly go to the bears."

I stared at him. "Why?"

His voice was heated when he replied, "Because a werewolf without a pack isn't a wolf at all. We need each other to survive, to give us purpose, to exist for something other than ourselves. Without the Pack, we're nothing."

I shook my head. "Do you hear yourself? I've survived sixteen years without a pack of werewolves. You know why? It's because I have friends! And they have my back just like I have theirs. They may not be werewolves, but they're the only pack I need." I motioned toward the canyon. "I don't need this, but do you know why I'm doing it? I need to survive to free my best friend."

"The vampire?" Ross asked with a tone of disgust at the word. He had lowered himself to sit on the edge of the wall as we talked

I nodded. "That vampire has saved my life many times, and I have saved his. We've bled together, been tortured, chased, stabbed, and burned, but we're still here because we've got each other's backs."

For a moment, I saw through the stalwart wall that Rhett hid behind. His dark gaze flickered and the bravado that held his shoulders back and made him appear confident slipped.

"You might have all that," he said quietly, "But we don't. Our only chance at a real life is to receive the brand and be accepted into the Pack." The wall came back up and he glared from me to Ross. "In order to do that, we need to survive the flood. I'm going down." He grabbed the rope and swung over. "It's your funeral if you choose to stay up here."

I watched them climb down several feet before I eased myself over. It wasn't like I actually had a choice. I may have had a pack back at the Academy, but I wouldn't be returning to it if I didn't survive the flood. The last thing I wanted to experience was being fed to bears. I had already faced one demon-possessed bear in my lifetime, and one was more than enough.

True to Rhett's word, the floodgates on the dam opened the moment our feet hit the ground. The roar of the raging water echoed so loud within the canyon walls I had to fight back the urge to cover my ears.

"Find something to grab onto," Rhett told Ross and me. He met my gaze. "And whatever you do, don't let go until we've gotten past the first rush. You'll be swept under by the debris."

He grabbed the trunk of a twisted tree that grew at the base of the canyon wall. Ross ran to the other side and did the same. Panicked and with nowhere to run, I found a thick root that had pushed its way through the wall at about shoulder height. I grabbed the root with both hands and gritted my teeth.

Within seconds, the wall of water was upon us. The raging, twisting, rushing wave carried trees, bushes, branches, dirt, leaves, and anything else that it swept up along its course. A huge trunk thicker than I was tall swept past inches from my face, and then the water crashed over me.

It took every ounce of strength I possessed to maintain my grip. The suffocating water pounded against me with the force of a dozen raging bears. Branches battered me from side to side and a trunk slammed into my head so hard my skull rebounded off the rock wall behind me. Dazed, it was only the fact that I had slipped my arm through the root and held it with my other hand that kept me there.

Sometime during the pounding, I had let go of the last of my air. I had to breathe. The sensation of drowning wasn't new to me, yet it carried the same panic-edged urgency of the night Sebastian drowned. Though the current was still too strong to fight, I was out of options.

I shoved away from the wall in what I hoped was an upward direction, but the moment I let go of the root, the force of the water sent me tumbling end over end. I swam, but didn't know which way was up. The debris that rushed around me flipped me in a summersault into a log with such force I lost what little remained of my breath. Water burned in my nose and my eyes could make out nothing through the mud-filled liquid. I clawed at anything I could reach.

Just past the log, my hand closed on something that didn't belong in the sharp tumble of debris. The texture was softer than the branches that scratched against me, but firm. I realized with a start that it was a foot. Following it down, I found that whoever it belonged to was trapped beneath the log. Scrambling with the last bit of strength I had left, I managed to free us both from the log.

Clear of the debris, I yanked backwards and the body followed. Glancing up through the dark haze that pressed against the edges of my mind, I saw a glimmer of light. I pushed off the log and dragged us both upwards.

My head broke the surface just before the darkness in my mind won. I sucked in a deep breath and coughed at the water I had gulped with it. I shoved the body up and went under again. With a final, desperate surge, I managed to grab the other person around the chest.

My watery gaze made out the side of the wall just feet away from where I struggled to keep our heads above the surface. With slow strokes impeded by the body I towed, I fought to reach the wall. Finally, my fingers brushed the rough side. The water carried us for several yards until I managed to snag the branches of a bush. My movements slow and exhausted, I inched the body out of the water onto the small outcropping where the bush grew. It felt like hours before I could pull myself up as well.

"Rhett," I said, my voice scratchy from breathing in the water. "Rhett, breathe."

A mouse wouldn't have heard my whisper.

Using the very last of my reserves, I slapped Rhett's bare chest.

"Breathe," I growled.

When the sound of his breath refused to meet my ears, I did the very last thing I could. I struggled to my feet on the little shelf and then collapsed on top of him. My shoulder hit his chest with such force that he started to cough. I pushed him weakly to his side and watched as he coughed out more water than he probably drank in a day.

"Breathe," I was finally able to bring myself to say again.

Rhett looked up at me. "Finn?" he said with confusion in his gaze.

I nodded. "You just survived the final Gauntlet."

Together, with slow, agonizing movements, we climbed to the top of the canyon and the group waiting beyond. I collapsed to my knees and watched Roundy run up and gather his son in a tight hug.

"I'm so proud of you!" the werewolf said. "You did it! You really did it!"

"That was amazing," another werewolf told Rhett.

"Good job," a woman said.

I caught several curious gazes and turned my attention to the ground in front of my knees. In the growing darkness, the earth looked soft and inviting.

I was contemplating curling up to sleep then and there when a hand touched my shoulder.

"You saved my son's life. How could I ever repay you?"

I looked up to find Roundy standing above me.

"A blanket?" I replied. My body shivered. I didn't know if it was from the freezing water we had just survived or if shock was setting in from what we had been through.

Roundy chuckled and helped me to my feet. "Get these boys some blankets!" he called out. He pulled me into a tight hug that surprised me. "Thanks for saving my boy. I don't know what I'd do without him," he said sincerely.

When he let me go, a woman wrapped a blanket around my shoulders.

"Come on, Finn," Rhett said from behind his father.

"Where are we going?" I asked.

Rhett smiled at me for the fist time since we had met. "Time to get branded."

Roundy and Rhett walked on either side of me. To my surprise, instead of returning to the Den for some sort of ceremony, the werewolves with Roundy had already started a fire. They moved so Rhett and I could get close enough to dry ourselves with the warmth.

After a few minutes interspersed with congratulations and teeth chattering, Roundy pulled something from the fire.

He held up a length of metal that glowed at the end in a shape that matched the wolf head on his forearm.

"Time to become a member of the Pack," he said to us.

Rhett gestured to me. "Finn first."

I shook my head. At his surprise, I said, "You've waited a lot longer for this."

With a grin that showed the gap in his teeth, Rhett held out his forearm. A hiss escaped him when his father pressed the brand to his arm, but he didn't pull away. When Roundy removed the brand and placed it back in the fire, the red, angry, raised mark on the boy's arm showed in stark contrast in the moonlight.

"It'll heal quickly," Roundy said, indicating the moon above us. "I'm proud of you, son."

"Thanks, Dad," Rhett replied. He turned to me. "You're next."

The thought of Vicken waiting chained and wounded with my brand as his only means of escape made me hold out my arm. I sucked in a breath when Roundy put the brand to it. His gaze traveled down my arm to the name written across the inside of my wrist.

"Who's Sparrow?" he asked.

"My dragon," I replied. At their surprised stares, I said, "She's with a friend right now."

A pang of sadness filled me as soon as the words left my lips. The baby sylph dragon who had chosen me on her hatching day and sacrificed herself to save my life had been with Alden when I left Haunted High to free my parents from monster killers, but she had vanished a few days before I returned. I had no idea where she was or how she was surviving in the city. I fought back the feeling of hopelessness at trying to find her. The only hope I had was that she would return to the Academy on her own. But how could a baby dragon ever hope to navigate such a huge city and return home?

"There," Roundy said, pulling the brand away. "Now it's official."

He handed the metal rod to one of his pack members and clapped Rhett and me on the back. "Welcome to the Pack, boys!"

Applause and cheers followed his words. The other members of the Pack were in the middle of their congratulations when headlights appeared further down the road. Two sets, then four, then a dozen trucks bounced up the dirt road at speeds far faster than should have been safe. The first truck slid to a stop near Roundy.

"What the—" he began.

"What's going on here?" Meg cut off when she shoved the door open and climbed out. A cloud of dirt puffed up when her shoes hit the ground. She slammed the door and stormed over to Roundy. "I demand answers!"

"We branded them," Roundy said with a grin. "They survived the Gauntlet. They're members of the Pack now."

"They're members of the Pack now," Meg repeated in a mocking imitation of his voice. "Did you see what I saw, Roundy, or did I miss something?"

"I-I don't know what you're talking about," Roundy said with a confused expression.

Meg looked back at the Pack members who were climbing out of the trucks to join her. "Did these two survive the Gauntlet according to all of the rules?" she asked.

Fear flickered on Roundy's face. I saw him take a step forward to place himself between Meg and his son.

"No," Stix said when he reached Meg's side. His face was hard when he continued with, "They didn't obey all of the rules."

"What are you talking about?" Roundy demanded. "Of course they did. They survived, didn't they? They're standing right here!"

A hint of sorrow brushed Meg's face only to disappear so fast when she looked at Rhett that I could have imagined it. "What happened under that water, Rhett? Did you swim to the surface all by yourself, and by yourself, did you climb onto that ledge to get free of the flood?"

I caught Rhett's intake of breath before he shook his head. "I was trapped. I-I couldn't get free from the log. I was drowning until—"

"Until what?" Meg prompted with a falsely sweet voice.

Rhett swallowed audibly and then said, "Until Finn managed to free me."

"That's right," Meg replied in the same sweet voice. "And what is one of the rules of the Gauntlet?"

Rhett hung his head. "No assistance is allowed."

Meg snapped her fingers. "Yes, that's it." She repeated his words in a singsong voice. "No assistance is allowed." She turned on Roundy and all mockery vanished to leave only steel in her gaze. "You branded them falsely, Roundy."

Roundy's eyes were clouded with tears when he shook his head. "No. They survived, Meg. You have to have a heart.

They deserve to be members of our Pack. They showed their strength. They were the only ones who survived!"

"Survived falsely," Meg spat. "I won't welcome cheaters into our Pack, and you did so knowing they broke the rules."

Her gun cleared its holster before Roundy could defend himself. Two shots rang out.

"Dad!" Rhett shouted.

He caught his father as Roundy collapsed to the ground. Blood trickled from the two holes in the man's chest. More blood spilled from where Rhett's hands clung desperately to his father's back. Roundy gave his son one last smile, and then his breath left him in a rattling gasp. Rhett could only stare as the life left his father's gaze and his head fell to the side.

Rhett turned hate-filled eyes on Meg. "You killed him!"

"You killed him when you broke the rules," she replied. She looked at me. "Just as you killed your vampire friend." Her gaze moved to the werewolves around us. "Stun them and throw them in the truck. They'll be bear food in the morning."

The thought of Vicken dying because of me made me reckless. I threw myself at Meg. I didn't know what I would do if I reached her. Instead of finding out, a bullet hit me in the back and dropped me to the ground. Rhett fell beside me. I closed my eyes against the sight of tears streaming from his dark gaze that was still locked on his father's face.

The hands that carried us into the back of the truck were gentle. The glimpses I caught of the faces of the werewolves around us showed their sorrow. It was obvious no one had thought the night would end like this. A woman with Lunera's long red hair sat in the corner of the truck with her face buried in her hands. A man rubbed her back as her shoulders shook. Other werewolves were also already in mourning. The thought that they had expected to welcome Ross and Durnin into their pack made me sad.

When we reached the Den, Rhett and I were thrown into the cage. I wondered if Meg had forbidden visitors because nobody even walked near the bars. Kiyah was conspicuously absent. I wondered if she would get in trouble for feeding Vicken. The thought that neither of us would survive the Den made me angry, but it was a futile, vain anger that had no outlet. Rhett lay in silence where they had set him. Though I heard his quiet sobs, I knew there was nothing I could do to ease his pain. I wish Dara was there to help, then retracted the thought. At least the girl I loved was safe.

When the numbing effects of the stun bullet lifted, there was nothing to do but sit and wait. Our thick handcuffs left us with few options. I couldn't help thinking of every step of the Gauntlet again. Guilt at what Rhett had gone through pressed against me.

"I'm sorry about your father," I said quietly.

Rhett glanced at me. His dark eyes were red, but he appeared to be out of tears. "You're dying because you chose to save my life."

"If we did it again, I would still pull you from that river," I replied.

Rhett watched me silently for a moment before he said, "Even if it means being eaten by bears?"

"Does it have to be bears?" I replied. At the shadow of a smile on his lips, I nodded. "Even then."

He sighed and shook his head. "It doesn't make sense."

I waited in silence for him to continue. When he did, his words gripped my heart.

"Why are we supposed to fight for each other and live for each other if to do so during the Gauntlet means death?"

I lifted a shoulder. "I think someone has too much power here."

"Meg," he whispered in a tone thick with anger.

I nodded. “For a people whose motto is to follow hierarchy, it doesn’t make sense to put someone in power who is the same rank.”

Rhett glanced at me. “We need an Alpha.”

I shook my head. “What you need is a fair government where everyone’s voice is heard. She’s grown too attached to her power, and so she gets rid of those who threaten her position.”

“Like us,” Rhett said with realization dawning on his face.

I nodded. “Like us.”

Footsteps sounded down the hallway. Ten armed werewolves appeared.

“Is it morning?” Rhett asked. He made a show of glancing at the windows above. “Still looks dark to me.”

One of the werewolves unlocked the cage. The door swung open with a creak.

“I’m sorry about this, Rhett,” the werewolf told him.

“You were brave out there, boy,” a woman said to me as she hooked a chain to my handcuffs.

“We’re praying for a quick death for both of you,” another told us.

“That’s reassuring,” Rhett said dryly. “I’m sure that’ll help.”

He shot me a nervous grin. I returned it. We would go out bravely and without tears, at least until we saw the bears.

That thought solidified when we were led to a thick metal door embedded in the wall. Stix waited next to it.

“I’ll see that your father’s body is properly laid to rest,” he told Rhett.

“I would rather you’d have fought for him,” Rhett replied, his gaze level.

Shame filled Stix’s face before he lowered his eyes to the floor. He pulled the door open without a word.

“Unlock their handcuffs,” a werewolf instructed.

The cuffs were unlocked. The guns of the werewolves kept me from entertaining the impulse to fight back. With my heart thundering in my chest to bely the calm expression on my face, I stepped inside. Rhett's shoulder brushed my own. We both waited until the door closed and was locked behind us. For a moment, the light was shut out, leaving us in total darkness. The musky, pine-tinged scent of bears flooded my nose.

"Ready for this?" Rhett asked.

"No," I replied. "You?"

"Definitely not."

Lights flickered on. My first glimpse was of a cavern lined with cameras. They apparently wanted to get a good view of our deaths. I had no doubt Meg required every werewolf in the Den to attend our slaughter. It was disgusting.

"Let's give them a good show," I said, stepping forward.

"I'd rather not give them a show at all," Rhett replied with a hint of nervousness in his voice.

A growl rumbled through the cave to cut off my reply. Scents of hunger, anger, and frustration wafted from a tunnel on the far side of the cavern. I felt the fall of heavy paws on the floor through my bare feet. Great snuffling sounds preceded a massive head that poked from the darkness into the light of the cavern. The huge brown bear blinked its beady eyes as its head swayed from side to side.

Chapter Six

"WHERE DID THEY GET these bears?" I asked as the one in front of us lumbered out of its cave. It was easily twice the size of the possessed bear Vicken and I had run from in the Academy forest. It lifted its head to sniff again. The hunger in its gaze was unmistakable. It focused on us and let out an earsplitting roar that made both of us cover our ears.

"We're in trouble!" Rhett said.

"Tell me about it," I replied.

A second bear followed the first. Soon, there were four massive bears watching us from in front of the tunnel. One licked its chops. It was easy to see how hungry they were. Instead of thick, healthy bellies, and full coats, these bears were gaunt with scraggly fur and a scent of desperation. The question wasn't if we were to be eaten, it was which bear would get to us first.

"Should we phase to wolf form?" Rhett asked with fear in his voice.

I shook my head. "Wolves will fight bears like predators. We need to think strategy."

A bear charged.

"My strategy is to run!" Rhett shouted.

He took off to the right. The bear seemed to think he was the most tempting morsel of the two of us because he moved in a lumbering gallop after the werewolf.

His actions fueled the other bears. Rhett's circuit around the circular cave sent him back toward the animals. He glanced at the two bears behind him. Desperation must have fueled their strength, because they were gaining on him. With two bears in front and two behind, Rhett was quickly running out of options.

I looked around the cavern, but there was nothing I could use as a weapon against the animals. Maybe Rhett was right. If phasing was the only chance we had to defend ourselves, at least we would go out fighting.

I reached for the wolf side of me and was about to phase when the biggest bear lunged at Rhett. Given his size and proximity, I was about to see the werewolf be torn in half.

"No!" I shouted and pushed at the same time.

It felt as though the seconds slowed. The bear paused with its jaws open and claws raised, Rhett slid to a stop in front of the other bears, and the last bear behind him turned and gave me its full attention. For that instant, every creature in the room waited for me to act.

A tremor ran over my skin. I sucked in a breath. My hands were up. I couldn't remember when I had lifted them. My fingers tingled the way they did when I pushed memories at someone. Only instead of memories, I had pushed a command.

I swallowed and said, "Back up." I pushed the thought along with speaking it, sending the bears an image of backing away from Rhett.

Rhett also backed up and almost tripped over the biggest bear.

"Not you, Rhett," I said.

He stopped, his expression confused. The bears also stopped. I felt the intense stares of each of them.

"Rhett, come here," I said as I pushed, "Bears, stay."

I could only stare as Rhett obeyed and the bears didn't move. Relief filled me when Rhett was far enough away to not be eaten.

He reached my side and then stared back at the bears. "What did you do?"

"I don't know," I replied honestly.

Rhett's eyes widened. "Finn, you compelled me. I had to do what you said."

"What are you taking about?" I replied, still trying to get my mind around what was going on.

"Finn," Rhett said breathlessly, "You're an Alpha!"

The bears ambled closer. I only had to hold out a hand and say, "Stay," for them to stop.

"They listen to me because I'm an Alpha?" I asked.

"I guess so," Rhett replied. "I've never met an Alpha before. I don't know what you can do."

"There's only one way to find out," I replied.

I walked toward the bears. When one opened its mouth, I pushed an image of what I wanted it to do. The biggest bear closed his mouth, watched me for a moment, then lowered to the ground. The other bears did the same. With my heart pounding so loud I was sure the spectators could hear it through the cameras, I stretched out my hand toward the closest bear.

Projecting images of calm, I set a hand on the bear's wide forehead. It merely watched me, its breathing steady and the look in its eyes more curious now than angry. Under my touch, the bear's eyes closed. After a moment, it turned its chin up so I could scratch beneath it. A smile spread across my face at the satisfied grunt the bear gave when I took my hand away.

"That's incredible," Rhett breathed.

He walked quietly up behind me and stretched out his own hand. The bear snapped his fingers.

He scooted back behind me. "Okay, uh, well, we know it's not me," he said. "You just, uh, keep them calm while we find a way out of here."

An idea struck me. I had no clue if it would work, but given the thickness of the metal door we had walked through, they could just starve us to death along with the bears. I wouldn't put it past Meg.

I projected calmness toward the bears and Rhett. The werewolf's nervousness around the animals was likely to set them off again. Each of the bears settled quietly on the ground with its eyes on me. I watched them out of the corner of my eye when I turned to face the camera.

"What are you doing?" Rhett asked from behind me.

"Everyone is watching us, right?"

"Yes," he replied. Bitterness showed in his voice when he said, "They're waiting to see us get eaten."

"Not if I can help it," I replied. I chose a camera and glared at it. Pushing with all of my might, I said, "You will unlock this door and let us out."

"Is that going to work?" Rhett asked.

I ignored him and lifted my hand. Pushing the command down my fingers the same way I sent memories, I repeated, "You will unlock this door and let us out."

Rhett and I turned our attention to the door. After a few minutes, the werewolf's shoulders slumped. One of the bears rose to its feet. I was about to face them again when a sound outside the door made me jerk back around.

"It's opening," Rhett whispered as if saying the words louder would jinx it.

I wondered who my compulsion had worked on. Expecting to see one or two werewolves, my heart leaped into my throat when the door was flung wide to reveal werewolves packed down either side of the hallway so thick there was barely standing room.

Rhett's wide gaze turned to me. "They. All. Listened."

I felt as if I was living a dream when I made my way to the door and the werewolves parted without a word.

Stix cleared his throat and then lowered his gaze when I looked at him.

"What about the bears, um, Sir?"

The title caught me by surprise. I fought back the edge of manic laughter that threatened to undo everything I had accomplished. A glance behind me showed that the four bears had followed close behind Rhett. When they poked their heads out of the cavern, the werewolves quickly fell back.

"Lock them inside," someone suggested.

"No," I said louder than was necessary. I had been in too many cages to turn my back when other creatures were suffering. I put my hand on the biggest bear's head. "They're coming with me."

Everyone fell back at my pushed order. My heart hammered in my throat and the voice in the back of my mind warning that everything could turn on me in a second. I willed my breathing to slow and turned to walk up the hallway with one hand on the massive bear's head and Rhett on my left side. The sound of the other bears' shuffling footsteps were followed after a respectful distance by the hundreds of werewolves.

"This is amazing," Rhett whispered.

I couldn't have agreed more, but I didn't dare to admit it. It felt as though I kept control by a tenuous thread that would snap if I lowered my guard for one second. Strangely enough, I felt safer with the bears than with the adult werewolves who walked around us with brands on their forearms that matched my own.

The realization that Meg hadn't been with the group that released us from the cavern hit me as soon as we stepped out of the tunnel and into the open arena. Meg waited with twelve armed werewolves on either side of her. The guns they pointed directly at me were no joke, and each guard had his or her finger on the trigger just waiting for Meg's command.

"Where do you think you're going?" she asked.

I ignored her and focused my attention on the guards standing on her right side.

"Lower your weapons," I said with a push.

The guards immediately obeyed.

"What are you doing?" Meg demanded.

I turned my attention to the guards on her left. "Lower your weapons."

"Don't you dare!" Meg said with an edge of panic in her voice.

The guards did as I commanded without even looking at her.

"If Meg goes for her guns, shoot her," I commanded.

Every guard turned to face Meg.

Meg looked at me. "What's going on here?" she demanded.

I stepped forward. The bears and Rhett followed, but I stopped them with a gesture. I continued toward Meg alone. Her hands twitched near her holsters, but she knew better than to draw.

I stopped about two feet from her. "Meg, I understand the hard work you have put into this place. You built a Den where werewolves could be safe and protected from the dangers of the world."

She opened her mouth, but I cut her off with a shake of my head.

"But the problem with the kind of power you've gained here is that it's easy to keep too much control for the sake of control instead of for the sake of keeping your pack safe."

Meg shook her head. "I did this to protect them."

My voice was calm when I replied, "Meg, you killed children on the pretense of doing so for the good of the Pack."

Meg sputtered. "But I didn't! We need our werewolves to be strong."

"But not strong enough, right?" I replied.

Meg stared at me. "What does that mean?"

I watched her closely. "You know exactly what I mean. If one of your young werewolves starts to show signs of being an Alpha or commanding the respect of the other werewolves, you set him or her up to fail." I motioned in the direction of the Gauntlet. "No one is supposed to survive this new and improved Gauntlet, are they?"

I heard the werewolves surrounding us, waiting for Meg's answer.

"Of course they are," she began.

I shook my head. "I was out there, Meg. The odds of survival without assistance was impossible." I glanced back at Rhett. "Rhett might have been able to save Lunera on the wall, but he couldn't because he knew it would break the rules, and now she's dead." The guilt in the boy's eyes was enough of an admission of truth for me to continue with, "And who knows? Maybe if Durnin had been able to have help or followed one of us through the tunnel of saws, he might be here with us right now." A sob from someone within the crowd said that he was mourned. "And when I saved Rhett's life, you shot his father and then threw us in with the bears."

I crossed my arms in front of my chest. "What good is being a werewolf if we can't rely on our pack? Isn't that what you teach here? Isn't that the point of the Den, so that werewolves can have each other's backs to protect? Then why isn't it allowed in the Gauntlet?" I met her gaze with a glare. "It's because you're afraid of those who show leadership abilities. You're afraid they'll take over the Den and be a better leader than you are." She opened her mouth to argue, but I cut her off with, "You preach about hierarchy, but you're afraid to follow."

I looked around us and met the gaze of every werewolf I could. I lifted my hands to push when I said, "From now on, no one is to follow Meg's rules or her commands. The Den can still be a place of safety, but it is not a dictatorship. You run your own families and see to their safety."

I met the gazes of several of the teenagers who had come to the cage. "As for your youth," I said with another push, "Those who are ready to break free of the laws and iron fist under which they've been governed will come with me to The Remus Academy for Integral Education where they will be welcomed as students." Several adults began to protest, but I raised a hand. "Parents are welcome to stay in contact with their children and can visit them if their children so wish." I looked around with steel in my glare. "But none of you can stop those who choose to leave the Den of their own free will."

I met Meg's astonished gaze. "Being weak physically shouldn't be a crime," I told her. "Everyone here has something to offer. At the Academy, your youth will have a chance to find their own path in this world that isn't dictated by the fear of failure. A pack should be made up of members with strengths in a variety of ways, not just physically. Compassion, intelligence, tenacity, book smarts, street smarts, and positivity all have their place in this world. It's time you realize that you can't shape your children; instead, you should respect the shape they give themselves."

"But will they come back?" a woman asked. Her hand rested protectively on the shoulder of the boy in front of her. An old bruise marked his cheek. I had seen enough of the Den to know that corporal punishment was the method of choice.

"They'll come back when they choose," I replied, my voice level. "But when they do, I suggest working out a new way to communicate rather than violence."

"We're going with him!" a girl whispered from behind me.

"We get to leave!" another said.

A boy of about ten near Meg grabbed the hand of the girl next to him who appeared to be his sister. "We're going," he said.

She nodded with excitement in her eyes.

I lifted my voice. "Anyone who wants to go with me to the Academy has ten minutes to gather your belongings and say your goodbyes. I will meet you at the exit to the Den at that time." I met the gaze of two of the werewolves with guns. "Bring food for the bears. They deserve to be fed."

Teenagers hurried from the crowd. Their parents trailed after them. Several argued with their children or pleaded for them to stay, but I wasn't surprised at those who rushed to get away. They had just seen several of the youth they no doubt looked up to be brutally slaughtered in the Gauntlet. The fact that they had lived their entire lives with the knowledge that they, too, would follow in their friends' footsteps must have been a heavy burden to carry. It was time that they were introduced to a world where there was a place for their strengths as well as weaknesses.

I met Meg's gaze again. The anger and defiance on her face was unmistakable. I knew only the fact that her own guards were ready to shoot her kept her from drawing her guns.

"I should throw you to the bears," I told her. "No creature should live in such conditions."

The biggest bear nudged his nose under my arm. I ran my hand across his massive head. "But they're coming with me." Thoughts of the forest through one of the Academy doors made me smile. "I know the perfect place for them." I took a steeling breath and gave one last push as I spoke to Meg. "You will remain here at the Den and strive to make up for the children whose lives you cut short at the Gauntlet. The cage is no longer a place of punishment and will be destroyed. Whipping is abolished, and the werewolves here will choose their own leaders through a yearly vote with the focus on the good of the Pack." Werewolves nodded around me. "Meg, power has turned you into someone who is cruel and unfeeling. Because of that, your job is to dismantle the Gauntlet completely."@

"But it's part of my life's work," she began.

I held her gaze and pushed, "You will dismantle the Gauntlet."

Her mouth closed and she nodded.

I held out my hand. "Give me your cellphone."

She pulled it from her pocket and handed it to me.

I turned away without another word and headed for the room where Vicken was being kept. Thoughts of my friend made me walk faster until I was nearly running. At the sounds that followed, I glanced back to see that the bears and a majority of the werewolves were also behind me. I ran through the halls Kiyah had shown me and slowed only when I reached the locked door.

"Open it," I told Stix.

He fumbled through his keys, then unlocked the door and pushed it open. My heart slowed at the sight of Vicken still chained to the table with Kiyah curled up at his side.

"Kiyah!" Stix called out before rushing to her.

The girl's head lolled when he picked her up frantically in his arms. A sheen of sweat showed on her face.

"Wha-what's happened to her?" her father asked.

I glanced at the bandage on her wrist. "She gave blood to Vicken. It's made her sick. She needs fluids and rest."

"She can stay," Stix said quickly. "I'll see that she has everything she needs. I can—"

"No," I replied. I had made Kiyah a promise and I was determined to keep it. "She'll be treated at the Academy. The infirmary there is set up for situations like these."

"But—" Stix began.

I met his gaze. "She's coming with me."

Stix lowered his eyes and nodded.

"Place her on a bear," I instructed. "She'll be carried to the exit." I knelt next to Vicken's still form. His face was a sickly gray and the wound from the bullet that had hit his forehead hadn't healed even with Kiyah's werewolf blood. He was in serious trouble. "Help me put Vicken on a bear as well."

I walked beside the great beast with a hand on the vampire's arm. He swayed with the bear's gentle movements, but gave no sign of awakening. The sluggish sound of his heartbeat made me anxious.

The two numbers I dialed on Meg's cellphone by heart were quickly answered. By the time the bears and I reached the exit from the Den, nineteen teenagers and five preteens waited with bags packed.

I turned back to their parents and the rest of the werewolves who watched us leave. "I'm not stealing your children," I said to reassure those with tears on their cheeks. "I am giving them a chance to see that there is more to the world than the Den. They can choose to come back, you can visit them at the Academy, and you yourselves are free to move from here if you wish." I met the gazes of several mothers and fathers who held children too young to come with me. "As your little ones reach school age, they will be welcome at the Academy to begin their education. There, they will be safe, respected, and have friends whose differences are also strengths." I glanced at Stix. "It's time we realize that our actions have a far greater impact than in just our small piece of the world. I know it's not easy to let your children go, but I will do everything in my power to keep them safe."

"Don't go," a woman with gray hair urged. "Stay with us. You're our Alpha."

"Yes, stay," a man with a thick blonde beard urged. "We need your guidance."

I could see the loss of everything they had known on their faces. I had just changed their lives completely. Their foundation that was based on Meg, the Gauntlet, and the walls that kept them safe, had been broken down. They were so used to following that taking their leader had left them in shock.

"I'm only sixteen," I said apologetically. "I don't know any more about a leading a pack than any of you."

"But you're an Alpha, *the* Alpha," the first woman said.

"You don't need an Alpha," I replied. I lifted a shoulder and said, "In fact, you don't need werewolves in your lives." At their astonished protests, I said, "I lived the first sixteen years of my life without other werewolves. I thought I was alone. My best friends are a vampire, an empath, a Grim, a warlock, a witch, and a dragon. Imagine my surprise when I was kidnapped and brought here to meet all of you!" At my grin, a few of them chuckled.

"You have each other," I told them in a more serious tone. "That's more than I had starting out. Worry more about being a family than a pack. Hierarchy is only there for protection, and you already have safety here." I looked at the teenagers who waited behind me. "When your children come back, they're going to have a whole lot of insight into this world to share with you." I turned back to their parents. "Learn from your children and teach them what you know. Together, your pack will be much better off."

The rumble of vehicles caught my ear. I glanced over my shoulder to see a string of cars and trucks heading our way at a far faster pace than they probably should have been traveling.

"That's our ride," I told Stix. "Watch over this place. I'll have Kiyah call you when she's feeling better."

Stix nodded. "Thank you, Finn." His eyebrows pulled together and he gestured toward the teenagers and then the other werewolves. "For all of this. We have a lot to learn, but you've given us a start."

I smiled at him. "I have a lot to learn, too. Maybe someday I'll be a good leader, but for now, what I don't know is a lot more than what I do."

Stix smiled back. "Spoken like a true leader." He nodded at my forearm. I turned it over to look at the wolf head brand. "You'll always be a part of our Pack, Finn."

"Thank you," I replied.

Chapter Seven

I TURNED TO FACE the approaching vehicles. The first one, a big black SWAT-looking truck, was very familiar. It skidded to a stop in front of the students. When Don and Donessa Ruvine left their vehicle with the grace and elegance of their vampire race, the teenagers around me fell back.

"Where's Vicken?" the Don demanded without formality.

Used to his straightforward ways, I replied, "He's here." At my push, the bears made their way through the werewolves and stopped in front of me. Vicken's unconscious form on top of the biggest one looked even paler in the sunlight.

"My boy," the Donessa said with a gasp.

At my motion, the bear lowered. The Don helped me ease Vicken off the bear's back. As soon as we were clear of the animal, Don Ruvine picked his son up in his arms and carried him to the truck.

"Thank you for bringing him back to us," the Donessa said with tears in her eyes. She set a hand on my cheek. "You're a good kid, Finn."

"Please have him call me when he wakes up," I said. The thought that I couldn't go to the mansion with Vicken and see to his recovery made my heart hurt. He had put everything on the line to rescue me from my kidnappers, and he had paid heavily because of it.

"I will," the Donessa promised. Her gaze turned to Kiyah who was being helped from one of the other bears by Rhett. "This is the girl who gave him blood?"

I nodded. "She's suffering from the effects. She needs liquids and rest."

"We can see to her care," the Donessa replied, surprising me.

I stared at Vicken's mother. "She's a werewolf."

The Donessa nodded. "I've learned to be a bit more openminded when it comes to werewolves."

That made me smile. "Thank you."

Rhett followed the Donessa to the vehicle. I walked around to the other side where Don Ruvine was busy ensuring the comfort and safety of his son. An I.V. had already been placed in Vicken's arm by another vampire and the bed he was strapped to in the ambulance-like SUV appeared secure. It hurt to see Vicken unresponsive even to his father's care. The fear that his head wound could be lethal pressed against my mind. I shied away from the thought. If anyone could help Vicken, it was his family.

"Take care of him," I told the Don needlessly before I was able to stop myself.

Don Ruvine straightened from checking the straps and faced me. "I will. You take care of yourself."

"I will."

His gaze sharpened as he looked me up and down. "Are you sure you don't want to come back to the mansion for some care yourself? You appear to have had a rough time here."

Rough didn't describe the half of it, but I didn't want to get into the details. The fact that Vicken's father was speaking to me in a fatherly, concerned tone told of how much our relationship had progressed.

"I'm fine," I told him. "But thank you." I looked back at the teenagers who watched us. "I have some friends to introduce to the Academy."

"Are they all werewolves?" the Don asked levelly.

I nodded. "How do you think that'll go over?"

The hint of a smile touched the Don's face. "I just wish I could be there to see it."

I smiled. "You're the lucky one." My smile fell. "Please let me know how Vicken's doing."

"I will," he reassured me with a stately nod. "He will hopefully be fit to call you soon."

"I hope so," I replied.

Other vehicles slowed behind the vampires. Professor Briggs stepped out of the first car.

"Don Ruvine," he said with a respectful bow of his head.

"Trace Briggs," the Don replied. He glanced at the werewolves behind me. "You're going to have your hands full, Professor."

"You just wish you were the one teaching," Briggs shot back.

The Don gave a regal nod. "As much as I'm sure they're afraid of you, they would be terrified of me."

Briggs' grin deepened, highlighting his scar. "You say it like that's a bad thing."

The Don smiled a true smile before he climbed into the back of the SUV with Vicken and his wife. A vampire shut the door, then drove them away.

Professor Briggs used his cane to limp to me. "Are you alright?"

The last time I had seen the professor, his anger at me for defending Uncle Conrad had made me wonder if he would ever forgive me. That thought vanished at the concern in his voice.

"I'm fine," I told him.

His eyes narrowed. "Finn," he said in a tone that let me know he guessed more than I had told him over the phone.

"I'm alright for now," I hedged. "But my friends need a ride to the Academy."

His gaze flickered over my shoulder and his eyes widened. "These are all werewolves?"

I fought back a laugh at the fact that it was everyone's first question. "Yes, all of them. And they're coming back to Haunted High with us."

The professor studied the group who waited nervously near the huge front door of the Den. The unease that wafted from the werewolves filled me with sympathy.

"Professor, they're choosing to leave everything they know to go to the Academy. They need a little compassion," I told Briggs.

The professor narrowed his eyes at me. "When have I been lacking in compassion?"

At my look, he gave a smile that twisted the scar down his cheek. "Fine, Finn. I can have compassion, believe it or not."

"I'll believe it when I see it," I replied.

"Finn!"

"Dara?"

I turned at the sound of her voice. Dara practically flew from a car driven by Mercer. The empath didn't slow and instead ran into me full force so that I had to catch her in my arms to avoid being bowled over. She kissed me soundly.

"I was so worried about you!" she said when her feet touched the ground again.

Professor Briggs cleared his throat.

Dara threw him a knowing look. "Don't even pretend to be appalled at our kiss, Professor. I can feel that you're more amused than anything."

Briggs actually chuckled. "I never thought Finn would find a girl that could put up with him."

Dara grinned as she stepped away from me. "He might surprise you, Professor."

"He already has," the professor replied.

Headmistress Wrengold reached us. The older woman's gray curls were tamed by a red and gold shawl. Her simple housecoat with the pocket watch on a gold chain and the matching brown dress pants made her appear modest but dignified. She stopped near me, gave a nod of welcome, and turned her attention to the werewolves.

"My name is Headmistress Wrengold, and I am in charge of the students that attend The Remus Academy for Integral Education," she introduced.

The smile she gave the teenagers was kind. I could see them warming to her and remembered feeling the same trust toward the Headmistress the first time I met her. The realization that she was far more equipped to lead them than I was eased some of the anxiety I felt about their wellbeing.

"I don't know if Mr. Briscoe mentioned that we have had a rocky relationship with werewolves in the past," she continued, "But we have since survived that hardship and have learned enough about each other to ensure that our relationship is a good one. That being said," she opened her arms in a sweeping gesture. "The Remus Academy for Integral Education would like to welcome you as students of our esteemed school."

The werewolves cheered along with some of their parents, which surprised me. Perhaps not everyone had been thrilled about Meg's leadership.

The Headmistress gestured behind her. "Please choose a vehicle to ride in. We look forward to showing you our Academy."

"Should we tell them it's haunted?" Dara whispered.

I grinned at her as we watched the students rush past us. "They'll find out soon enough."

"Professor Briggs, Mr. Briscoe, I request your company on the trip back," the Headmistress said in a tone that left no room for argument. She smiled at Dara. "And you are welcome to join us, Ms. Jade."

"We need somewhere the bears can ride," I said.

The Headmistress looked from me to the bears that lounged near the students.

"The bears are coming with us?"

I nodded. "They can't stay here. They've been starved and used to eat werewolves who fail the Gauntlet. They deserve a peaceful life."

"In the forest?" the Headmistress guessed.

I was grateful she didn't ask about the eating werewolves part. I nodded. "I thought they would be alright there."

She considered it, then nodded as well. "They will, but I don't know how well the animals will ride in a vehicle."

"They'll do just fine," I replied. I lifted a hand to the animals. "Come on, bears. Time to go home."

I felt the surprised stares of my professor, the Headmistress, and my girlfriend when the bears rose and crowded around me. Each one appeared eager to get his or her head scratched, and I was happy to oblige.

When Rhett opened the door to the moving truck I had ridden in to the Gauntlet, the bears needed only a slight push to climb inside. They seemed as eager to leave the Den as the teenagers were.

"Is there an explanation for this?" Professor Briggs asked.

I nodded and looked at the Headmistress. "Somebody once guessed that I was an Alpha. It took being confronted by bears driven vicious through starvation for me to believe it."

The Headmistress gave a single nod with a proud smile. "I took a chance on you, Mr. Briscoe. I can honestly say I never guessed where that would lead us."

"The students who haven't had a chance to be put to the Gauntlet are grateful," I replied. Sadness filled me when I thought of Lunera, Durnin, and Ross. "But others will never have the chance to grow up away from that kind of fear. Thank you for trusting me enough to give them the opportunity."

The Headmistress nodded. "Let's go home."

I smiled. "I like the sound of that."

The adult werewolves waved at their children as the vehicles pulled away. Tears showed on some faces while pride was visible others. I couldn't help wondering how much life would change at the Den now that Meg was no longer in charge. Perhaps things would go back to the way they were before I was brought to the Den, but I hoped not. At least the Gauntlet wouldn't be used with the teenagers gone. They would have a lot of restructuring to do. I was glad the younger werewolves were gone from the chaos.

The seats inside the SUV faced each other like a limousine. By the scent, it was the Headmistress' own vehicle, though Mercer was the one who drove. Relief at seeing the gruff Mage away from his bed in the infirmary swept through me. He nodded when I climbed into the vehicle.

"Didn't think I'd see you alive," he said in his low, gravelly voice. His customary expressionless face didn't reveal how he felt about the statement.

"I thought the same about you," I replied.

He gave a grunt that could have been laughter before he followed the caravan of vehicles away from the Den. My shoulders slumped against the seat. With Vicken cared for, the Gauntlet gone, and the Den fading away in the distance, I felt as though I could finally breathe. Dara's hand held mine and she traced patterns across the back of my arm as though she couldn't help touching me. A sigh of relief escaped me and won a smile from her.

The Headmistress spoke up several minutes after the Den had disappeared from sight.

"The gateway between our world and that of the demons is getting stronger," she said. "I am reluctant to bring new students to the Academy. If it wasn't for these extreme circumstances, I would have denied them until the demon problem was dealt with."

Her tone caught my attention. "What's going on?"

Professor Briggs spoke up. "Your team has been hard-pressed to keep the demons away from our school. Chutka knows we have the pieces of his heart and he's trying desperately to get them back before we destroy them. He knows his chance of gaining access into our world comes from those pieces."

"The werewolves can fight," I said. "They'll listen to me." I didn't point out that they had to. I was still getting used to the idea myself. I didn't want to take away anyone's ability to make their own choices.

"We can't put them in harm's way just after freeing them from what sounds like a terrible situation," the Headmistress said.

"If you heard what it's like at the Den, they're used to being in harm's way. They've been training for the Gauntlet since birth, pretty much. At least we know they're strong. They can be relied on," I replied.

Professor Briggs shook his head. "We didn't accept werewolves into the Academy as your own private army, Finn."

The implication smarted. "I know that, Professor. I'm just saying—"

"You're saying we can use them because they're students," Briggs replied. "I'm saying we *can't* use them because they're students. It isn't right."

I met his gaze. "I'm a student and I fought to protect the school."

"That was different," Briggs began.

"Because I was the only werewolf," I finished for him. I wasn't sure if it was the fact that I had survived death at least two more times in as many days, or the fact that their readiness to accept werewolves now after all I had gone through stung more than I was willing to admit, but I was done trying to play nice. "Professor, Headmistress, you're looking at this the wrong way. The werewolves are strong. They'll be willing to protect the Academy because it's all they have."

"You're wrong, Finn," Briggs replied sharply. "If I understand correctly about what they went through at the Den and this Gauntlet, you're asking them to prove themselves by using their strength to protect our school. How is that any different than the Gauntlet?"

"Because they're not going to die if they fail!" I shot back heatedly.

"Won't they?" Briggs asked, holding my gaze. "If we fail to keep Chutka from the Academy, we all die."

The starkness of his words stole a bit of my fire.

Dara set a hand on my back and I winced.

"What was that?" the professor asked, his gaze searching.

"Nothing," I muttered.

"Finn," Dara began.

Anger so hot and demanding surged through me I couldn't contain it. I turned and slammed a fist into the window next to me. It shattered, but the glass didn't fall out.

"Mr. Briscoe, contain yourself," the Headmistress scolded.

I lowered my gaze, embarrassed that I had lost my cool. "I'm sorry, Headmistress. I don't know what's gotten into me," I apologized.

"It's the heart," Mercer said with a glance in the rearview mirror.

Everyone looked at me.

"You feel it?" Dara asked.

I stared at her. "The pieces of the heart are here?"

Professor Briggs nodded. "We couldn't leave them at the Academy. Chutka's demons have been targeting us. It's the only way to keep the students safe."

"But the pieces are in ironwood," the Headmistress said. "You shouldn't feel their effects."

"But he does," Dara said. "I can feel it." She gave me an apologetic look. "I've felt your frustration grow the longer we've been in here. I thought it was just because you're healing, but—"

"Healing from what?" Briggs asked.

I couldn't take the silence that followed their words. I sighed and pulled off my shirt, then turned my back so they could see.

"Finn, are those whip marks?" Dara asked in shock.

I nodded. "Like I said, it's good we got the kids out of the Den. They're really into corporal punishment there."

I moved to put my shirt back on, but Briggs grabbed it. "When did you get those?"

I thought back. The days had really blurred together. "Three days ago, I think. I broke a few rules about not hurting members of the Pack." A grim smile crossed my face. "At least they won't forget anytime soon.

"Shouldn't that have healed by now?" Dara asked.

I nodded. "Yeah, but I got shot, then there was the Gauntlet, and then they tried to feed us to the bears. I also got branded," I said, holding out my arm to show them the wolf head. I forced a light tone when I said, "I don't think my body knows how to function right anymore." I took the shirt back from Briggs and slipped it over my head. "Life hurt a lot less when I was human."

The professor watched me closely. "Are you sure you're up to going back to the Academy?"

"Of course," I replied, surprised that he would even ask. "We need to stop Chutka, and I have some classes I'm so behind on you might have to hold me back for my entire life." I gave Headmistress Wrengold a pleading look. "Unless you have pity on me and grant school credit for killing demons."

She gave me a half-smile. "I'll consider it."

I looked at the professor. "How about credit in Black Cat Philosophies for discovering hundreds of werewolves no one thought existed?"

"How is that related to the class?" Briggs asked.

I lifted a shoulder. "They supposedly didn't exist and now they do?"

He shook his head. "I don't think you understand the concept of a philosophy."

I grinned at him. "I'd have to blame that on my teacher."

Briggs rolled his eyes.

Before he could reply to my sarcastic comment, the Headmistress surprised me by saying, "Finn, our students are poorly equipped to deal with the demons that are plaguing our school. If you can help us train them in demon defense, I'll grant you credit as an assistant professor."

I stared at her. "Really?"

"Really," she replied.

Professor Briggs stared at her as well, "Assistant professor?"

The Headmistress tapped him on the hand with one of her white gloved-fingers. "Don't look so surprised, Professor. You weren't much older than him when you took on a teaching position. Let's give him a chance."

Professor Briggs watched me for a moment before he said, "We're all in trouble."

I had to agree.

Chapter Eight

THE WEREWOLVES WERE MUCH better received at Haunted High than I had expected. I hoped I could take some credit for the lack of fear the other students showed, but it was really because the teenagers who came with me were just grateful to get out of the Den and were thrilled to meet other monsters. It reminded me of how I had felt when I realized I wasn't alone in the monster world. But as I watched the students mingle and get to know each other that night at dinner in the cafeteria, I felt a pang of sadness.

"What's wrong?" Dara asked quietly.

"Nothing," I replied. "I just, well…." I didn't know how to voice the way I felt. I swallowed the piece of chicken that had gotten lodged in my throat and said, "I guess I thought finding a pack would feel differently."

Dara gave me a knowing look. "They aren't your pack, Finn. You know that."

"We're your pack," Brack said from across the table.

I looked up in surprise. I hadn't realized the huge warlock had been listening. He and Lark had been busy telling about the demons we had captured in Lark's basement home, but while Lark regaled the younger werewolves with details of my clumsy run through the streets, it seemed Brack's mind was on other matters.

"We're your pack," he repeated. "And we have work to do."

I nodded. "Chutka's heart."

"Yes," Lyris said from Brack's other side. "It's time to destroy it."

I sat back. "What if I said I had a different idea?"

Dara gave me a wry smile. "I'd say if Vicken were here, he would tell you it was a bad one."

The thought of my best friend struggling to survive at the vampire mansion made my heart ache. I nodded through the pain. "Yes, he would, and he especially would if he heard it."

"Well," Jean, the blue-haired vampire from the defense team, prompted. "Out with it."

"Yeah," Lorne, the other vampire on our team said. "Don't keep us in suspense, Finn." He closed his black-gloved fingers into fists. "I'm ready to finish this demon lord once and for all."

"Demon Prince," Dara corrected.

Lorne rolled his eyes. "Whatever. Prince, lord, he needs to die."

"We can't kill him."

Everyone looked shocked at my statement. I clarified with, "Not yet. Not until we make sure every demon my uncle accidentally released into this world goes with him."

"I thought you said the Maes are going to start hunting demons," Alden pointed out.

I nodded at the Grim. "That's what they said, but I don't trust Madam Opal one bit. I give them a year to start monster hunting again."

"Why?" Lyris asked.

I lifted a shoulder. "Monster hunting is easier. They've been doing it for years, and those Maes members Vicken didn't inject with my blood can't see the demons. They're still a threat."

"Great," Dara grumbled.

I lifted a shoulder. "At least for now they're helping us fight." I smiled at Dara. "We've made a difference."

She didn't appear amused. "Finn, you're changing the subject."

I had hoped she wouldn't notice, but Dara knew me better than anyone. I toyed with the last piece of chicken on my plate and glanced around at the other monsters in the cafeteria. No one appeared to notice our little meeting. Laughter, loud conversations, and the sound of trays on tables and ringing utensils filled the air. Regardless, I knew we had to be careful. Alden had been possessed and used against us. Anyone at the Academy could potentially be a spy for the Demon Prince.

"Let's go to the basement," I said. "I need Professor Briggs and Mercer to weigh in on my plan." I hesitated, then suggested, "It probably wouldn't hurt to have the Headmistress there since this could affect the Academy."

"I'll get her," Lyris offered.

"Thank you," I replied.

"I'll get Briggs and Mercer," Alden said.

"And I'll bring Lark," Brack told us. He began to laugh, his deep voice echoing off the walls. "I'm funny," he said with a grin.

I chuckled as Lark burst into laughter. "And I'll bring Brack," she replied. They both laughed louder. It was good to see the witch fitting in.

"Alright. Let's meet downstairs in ten minutes," I told them.

Brack was right. It didn't matter how many werewolves filled the Academy. My pack was made up of vampires, witches, a warlock, a Grim, and an empath. But without Vicken, it didn't feel complete. I vowed to visit him as soon as we were done.

I had gotten into the habit of checking my phone every few hours since rescuing my family. As if on cue, my phone started to ring the instant I stepped into my room.

I hurried to it. No one called since they knew I couldn't bring it to class. Cellphones weren't exactly allowed at Haunted High, but so far no one had caught me. I picked up the phone, but the number wasn't one I recognized. I answered it anyway.

"Hello?"

"Finn?"

"Vicken!" Even weak, his voice was unmistakable.

"Hey, Finn. You okay?"

"You're asking if I'm okay?" I asked incredulously. "I thought you were going to die, Vick. I didn't know what to do."

Vicken grunted. "It was close," he admitted. He was quiet for a moment, then he said, "Kiyah saved my life."

"I know," I replied. "I couldn't get to you. They wouldn't let me. I'm so sorry." The words were hard to say. If it wasn't for Kiyah, Vicken would have died chained to the round table at the Den.

"Don't do that."

"Do what?" I asked.

"Don't you dare apologize. Kiyah told me what you did. She watched everything. She just finished telling me about it."

"And he insisted on calling you," a voice said, her words quieter than Vicken's as if she was further away.

"I'm having a conversation," Vicken said. "Werewolves shouldn't listen in even if they can. It's rude."

I grinned. Vicken was definitely feeling better.

"Then vampires shouldn't talk so loud," Kiyah replied.

"I like her," I said.

"You would," Vicken replied.

I could picture him rolling his eyes. But something to his tone caught my attention. "You like her," I said in amazement.

"No, I don't," Vicken denied.

"You do!" I said, catching the hint of embarrassment in his words.

"Why would I like a werewolf?" Vicken demanded.

I heard Kiyah laugh. "Because I don't put up with your garbage," she said.

"You can leave," Vicken told her.

"I know," she shot back. "But I won't. You're stuck with me until you can walk straight."

That made me worry. "You're having trouble walking?"

"Great," Vicken muttered. He raised his voice and said, "Now you've worried Finn. The last thing I want to do is worry him. He's impulsive and likely to do something rash."

"I can hear you," I told him.

"You can't get mad at everyone who cares about you," Kiyah said.

"I don't get mad—"

"Yes, you do," she replied, cutting him off.

"Stop cutting me—"

"Cutting you off?" she cut him off. "I only do it when you deserve it. You're worrying your friend and Mr. Ruvine said you need to rest. Now tell Finn goodbye."

"Bye, Finn," Vicken said sullenly.

I couldn't help grinning at how grumpy he sounded.

"Bye, Vick. I've got to go anyway. The team is waiting and—"

"What's your plan?"

I grimaced at the thought of how he would react. "Now who's cutting someone off?" I asked, stalling.

Vicken's tone was serious when he said, "Finn, tell me your plan."

I grimaced. "You're not going to like it."

"Sounds like nothing new," Kiyah said.

"Stay out of this conversation!" Vicken shouted.

Kiyah laughed, sounding as though she wasn't the least bit perturbed by his outburst.

"Don't worry," I told Vicken. "You need to rest. I'm sure things will be just fine."

"Finn, don't you dare—"

"Rest, Vicken. Don't worry. See you soon." I hung up the phone.

I imagined how angry Vicken was on the other end. It made me glad to be far enough away that I could avoid his wrath. I was sure it wouldn't be good for his healing process. Hopefully Kiyah would get him to calm down so he could focus on healing, but I doubted it.

The phone rang again. I toyed with the idea of ignoring it, but Vicken was stubborn enough to take one of his limos back to Haunted High to beat some sense into me if I didn't answer. I sighed and pressed the button.

"Hey."

"Don't 'hey' like everything's just fine," Vicken snapped. "You're going to a team meeting right now, correct?"

"Yes," I said cautiously.

"Take me with you."

I couldn't help laughing. "That sounds desperate."

"Finn," Vicken said in the tone that let me know he was on his last fragment of patience. "Put the phone on speaker and take it with you. I might not be there, but I'm going to participate in this meeting."

"That's ridiculous," I began.

Vicken cut me off. "This isn't negotiable. I'm a part of the team. I'm breathing—"

"Barely," Kiyah said.

"And I'm going to attend the meeting in whatever capacity I can," Vicken concluded, ignoring the werewolf.

"Fine," I replied. It was easier to agree than wind up with another half hour of arguing with the vampire. I could only imagine how the anger was impeding his healing. With any luck, the cellphone would lose reception in the basement and it would be a moot point.

Unfortunately, that wasn't the case. I ended up setting the phone in the middle of the thick wooden table that took up one end of the dark training room. Mercer eyed the phone, but his stony expression didn't let me know how he felt about it.

Alden, on the other hand, appeared tickled to have Vicken attend in any form.

"They told me what happened!" Alden said. "When I woke you up, I had no idea you'd go chasing after Finn. That was incredible!"

"Yeah, well, nearly dying didn't feel so incredible," Vicken grumbled.

"You're a hero," the Grim gushed. "That was so brave!"

I fought back a grin at the thought of Vicken getting shot the moment he pulled me from the car. I was sure somewhere in the back of his angry mind he was grateful I had left that part out.

"Whatever," Vicken said. "Let's begin this meeting."

"Yes," Headmistress Wrengold agreed from her seat at the top of the table. Her white gloved hands were crossed in front of her, appearing far out of place in the dark, dungeon-like basement. "This is a bit unusual, Finn. Why did you call us all here?"

I looked around at my team members, Professor Briggs, Mercer, and the Headmistress. Uncle Conrad sat next to Mercer looking entirely uncomfortable at the situation in which he found himself. Because he was the reason the gate had been opened in the first place, it was fitting to have him there. But after all he had been through, I was reluctant to involve him, or any of them, for that matter. My next words were going to ask a lot of everyone who sat around the table. I cleared my throat and said, "I don't think we should destroy Chutka's heart."

"What!" Lyris said in surprise.

"Why not?" Brack asked, confusion clear in his deep voice. "Chutka is bad."

"That's a stupid idea," Vicken shouted from the phone.

"Take it easy," Kiyah told him.

Arguing escalated around the table. I fought back the urge to quiet them with a shout. Everyone deserved to have their voice heard. I had to make them understand. If they didn't, our trouble was just beginning.

Only Professor Briggs sat quietly at the opposite end of the table from the Headmistress. The head of his cane hung from the table as a reminder of the damage Chutka's subordinates had already done.

"Why?"

The professor's quiet voice was a stark contrast to the heated arguing. The vampires were busy siding with Vicken, no surprise there. Lark had slipped her tiny hand into Brack's huge one for reassurance. The big warlock patted it comfortingly, but didn't look at all pleased by my words. Dara was arguing with Lyris about my decision, and Alden, Mercer, and the Headmistress appeared to be in the middle of a discussion about my sanity. Uncle Conrad's gaze was on the table. He refused to participate in any of the conversations or even look at me. It made me hurt to see him so filled with guilt at the situation in which he had placed us.

"Why?" Professor Briggs repeated just loud enough to catch the others' attention.

Even Vicken stopped talking. Everyone's focus turned to me.

I put my hands on the table. "Because Chutka isn't going to stop trying to come here."

"But if we destroy his heart, he can't get through," Lyris said.

"Maybe not right now," I replied. "But he'll never stop looking for ways."

"But if we trap him there, the school will be safe," Alden said.

"But for how long?" I asked.

"What do you mean?" the Grim replied.

I looked at each of them in turn. "Do you really think Chutka will give up if we destroy a few pieces of his heart?" I shook my head. "He wants this too badly."

"But if we destroy the pieces, he'll be out of options," the Headmistress said with a hint of hope in her voice.

I shook my head. "He may be weaker, but he'll never give up." I rose and looked at Uncle Conrad until he met my gaze. "How long until another angry student starts to meddle in dark magic?" When Conrad looked away, I turned my attention to the others at the table. "How long until someone here, either this current generation, or a generation years from now, gets fed up with the way monsters are treated in this world? How long until someone decides they've had enough and starts looking for the kind of power they need to make a difference?"

"Is that what Conrad was doing?" Alden asked in surprise.

I nodded. "It was a simple enough desire," I told my friend. "You've seen the way werewolves are treated. It wasn't much different back then." I glanced at my uncle. "It's not easy being part animal. Believe me. I know. But nobody else who hasn't been there could possibly understand." My hands clenched into fists. "Chutka thrives on unrest, on the need to make a change, on the want for enough power to make a difference. He's clever, and we need to remember that. Shutting him out right now isn't protecting our future or the future of our children."

Dara touched my hand. My fingers relaxed when hers interlocked with my own. I took a calming breath and told them my plan. "We're going to bring Chutka the Shambler to Haunted High."

"That is the stupidest plan you've come up with yet, Finn," Vicken said, his voice tinny over the phone's speaker.

"Thanks," I replied drily. "I try."

At least nobody was arguing. I had apparently stunned them to the point that everyone simply looked at each other and then me in amazement. I took advantage of the silence.

"Chutka is planning to destroy this world beginning with the people I love."

I looked down at Dara. She squeezed my hand. "How do you know?" she asked quietly.

"I saw it," I said. I was unable to suppress the shudder that ran down my spine. "Just before we killed the Darkest Warlock, I saw his memories. I saw Chutka give him the piece of his heart to tempt Conrad. I saw the Wiccan Enforcer and the Demon Knight locked in some sort of room. I saw millions of demons waiting to come to our world."

I let out a breath, then said, "And I heard Chutka's voice just before the Warlock died. He promised that he would come for those I love and destroy everything I care about." Dara's hand trembled slightly in mine. I tightened my hold on her fingers. "And he's coming. It might not be today or tomorrow, but he will find a way to breach the gate." I looked at my friends and teachers. "And I would rather it be now when we're prepared to deal with him rather than some time in the future when students have forgotten the threat demons pose or they have forgotten how to face them."

Silence filled the room. At least they weren't arguing against me. I could see the fear my words caused. The thought of Chutka the Shambler threatening the Academy once more made the Headmistress' face pale. Even Mercer appeared shaken out of his usual stalwart expression to the point that I caught the smallest hint of surprise in his gaze. Briggs gave one shallow nod which lessened the fear I held that they would tell me I was imaging things. At least the professor knew the threat would never leave until we banished it once and for all.

"Finn, I hate to say you're right, but you're right," Vicken said over the phone.

I couldn't hide the surprise that filled me. "Did you just agree with me?" I asked him.

"Don't get used to it," Vicken replied.

Headmistress Wrengold laced her fingers in front of her. "I suppose you have a plan?"

"Yes," I replied. "And I'm sure Vicken will like it."

The snort of derision that came from the phone said otherwise.

I gestured to the three boxes Mercer had placed on the table. They looked innocent enough. The ironwood of which they were made kept the power of Chutka's heart from affecting those at the table. I didn't want to think about how strong they would be if allowed to join back together.

"We're going to use Chutka's heart pieces to bring him here, and then give him his heart back," I said.

Vicken sputtered.

"You just spit your blood everywhere," Kiyah said with a note of disgust. "Stop drinking while Finn is telling you his horrible idea!"

"At least wait until I'm finished," I said. I looked at Dara. "Do you have the moonstone Madam Opal gave us?"

She nodded. "It's locked in Professor Brigg's room."

"Good," I replied. "We're going to bind the pieces of Chutka's heart with the moonstone before we give it back to him. My hope is that after it's in his chest, if we expose him to moonlight, the stone will overpower him and destroy him the way it destroyed the Darkest Warlock."

Mercer set his scarred hand on the table. "Let me get this straight," he said, his gravelly voice grating against my ears. "We bind the heart to the moonstone, summon Chutka here, give him his heart back, and hope that after he returns to full power the moonstone will destroy him? It sounds a little weak."

"It is," I admitted. "That's why we need the whole school."

Mercer's eyebrows actually rose. I had never seen that before.

"Hear me out," I said before anyone could argue. "We know Chutka's not coming alone. You should see the number of demons we trapped in Lark's home in the city."

"What?" Professor Briggs interrupted. "You trapped demons in the city?"

I cringed inwardly. "I think we forgot to mention that."

Vicken gave a wry chuckle over the phone.

"It's alright," Lark said. "They're comfortable. There's plenty of boxes."

Dara nodded. "They're good boxes, so don't worry."

Lark shot her a beaming smile.

"Why are we talking about boxes?" the Headmistress asked.

I lifted a hand. "Don't worry about the boxes. What's important is that the demons are trapped there and can't get out. The barrier Brack and Lyris created will hopefully last until we defeat Chutka."

"In which case, what happens to the demons?" Jean asked.

I met the blue-haired vampire's gaze. "I'm not sure. I've never defeated a demon prince before. But I'm hoping they'll vanish or something."

"Poof," Lark said with a giggle.

Brack grinned at her. "Poof," he agreed in his deep voice.

Professor Briggs shook his head. "There are too many unknowns here. It's too dangerous to involve the students. We need to send them home."

"No!"

Everyone stared at the phone.

Vicken spoke again, his voice fueled by anger. "No, Professor. Now is the time to end this. We've spent far too much time and energy trying to stop Chutka's followers. If we have a chance to cut off the head of the snake, we have to take it." He paused for a moment and I could hear his heavy breathing.

"Easy," Kiyah whispered. "Just take it easy."

When Vicken spoke again, his voice was quieter and his words weak as though his outburst had taken a lot out of him. "If we don't succeed, we risk endangering the school, but if we don't try, the entire world is already doomed."

Chapter Nine

I SAT DOWN WITHOUT speaking. The silence that filled the room this time was charged. Inwardly, I was grateful that Vicken was fighting the battle at my side. I held my breath, hoping the others would agree. I felt my tension ease and glanced at Dara. She gave me a small smile. I pushed gratitude toward her and her smile widened.

"We need to give the students the option," the Headmistress said. "They need to know the danger they will be facing, and be able to leave if they feel it is too much for them."

"That sounds fair," Professor Briggs replied. "But if they choose to go home, they shouldn't be allowed to return."

I stared at the professor and saw everyone else do the same.

"Why?" the Headmistress asked in a level voice.

Professor Briggs met my gaze. "If Finn has taught us one thing at this Academy, it's that a pack doesn't have to be made up of only werewolves or only vampires, or witches, or Grims, or whatever. Monsters need each other." His sat up in his chair and winced slightly at some unseen pain. "When this team freed monsters from the Mythic Labs, it started a ripple." He gave me a slight smile that pulled on the thick scar that marked his cheek. "You didn't know that, did you, Finn?"

I shook my head.

The professor nodded. "Well, it did. Monsters are banning together to protect their families. There is strength in numbers and safety in combining forces with those whose skills are different than our own." He waved a hand to indicate the world outside the Academy. "There are networks forming, meetings taking place, and tough conversations like this one occurring in which the attendees realize they can't survive on their own. Monsters are outnumbered and being different will always be a reason to be feared."

He opened his scarred hand. "But not here." His words were strong and filled with warmth. "At Haunted High, we are learning to trust each other. We are finding the value of friendship with those who are different. When I was a student here—" He paused and met Conrad's gaze. "When *we* were students here, nobody strayed outside of their own groups. Witches didn't converse with vampires. Warlocks stayed away from empaths, and everyone avoided the scary, unpredictable, instinct-driven werewolves." He winked at me. "But thanks to Finn, we're learning to be less afraid and more open to these differences. The students are growing in ways we struggled with. They're strong, and they're better able to deal with something like Chutka the Shambler. Thanks to Finn, I think we can handle it."

I shifted uncomfortably in my seat.

"That's giving Finn a bit too much credit," Vicken said with a grunt.

The professor turned his attention to the phone. "This coming from his best friend who happens to be a vampire. Tell me, Vicken, how many friends did you have before Finn arrived who weren't vampires?"

The silence that followed made the professor smile in triumph.

"Alright, your point is made," the Headmistress said. "But I don't agree with telling the students who leave that they can't return. The Remus Academy for Integral Education was created by my husband as a place of refuge for all students. They deserve to feel protected here. If they choose to go home until it's safe to return, we can't blame them. They are children, after all."

"Something we tend to forget," Mercer said gruffly.

Professor Briggs was silent for a moment with his eyes on the table. It was easy to see that it wasn't the table top but memories he watched with his distant gaze. When he spoke again, his voice was quiet. "Students deserve to feel safe. That's why we chose to become professors." He looked at the Headmistress. "You're right, Fanny. They should have a choice. And I won't stand in the way of their return. I'll encourage the other professors to do the same."

"Thank you," she replied.

"Then it's settled?" Vicken asked from the phone.

The Headmistress gave a nod that was filled with the weight of all she had just learned. "It's settled. We will assemble the students so that I can address their concerns. In the meantime, Professor Briggs, Mercer, and I will begin research into how to bind the heart to the moonstone. We'll teach the spell to the other professors." She looked at the students in turn. "Lyris, Brack, you will train the witch and warlock students on the shielding chants. Conrad, you need to brush up on those spells you used to unlock the gate in the first place." Conrad nodded wordlessly. "The rest of you will begin demon combat training under Finn. Please notify Mercer if you need the imitation flame for practice."

The thought of touching demon fire again, even the imitation flame Mercer kept in the box in the corner, made my hand throb. Though the skin had finally healed, I wasn't eager to expose myself to it again.

"What can I do?" Vicken asked.

The vampire's voice sounded small and frustrated coming from the phone.

A true smile touched the Headmistress' lips. "Vicken, you get back here as soon as you are healthy. We miss your charming personality."

Laughter followed the Headmistress' words.

"You should," Vicken replied with a huff. "I know you miss me."

I picked up the phone.

"We do," I told him honestly. "I can't imagine facing Chutka without you. Get better and get back here. There's a war coming."

"I'll be there," Vicken promised.

I hung up the phone.

"Well," I said. "Time to see what kind of warriors werewolves make."

"Don't you know?" Lark asked.

I shook my head. "I have no idea. I've personally just been pretending to be a werewolf up to this point. You should see these guys. They're the real deal."

"Pretending," Brack said. He grinned and repeated it. "Pretending to be a werewolf." He started to laugh his deep, rolling, echoing belly laugh. It was so contagious everyone in the basement caught on. Dara leaned her head on my shoulder as she laughed and even Mercer gave a grunt that could have passed for laughter from the sweep.

When Brack finally stopped, he patted me on the shoulder with a beefy hand. "You're funny for a werewolf, Finn."

I grinned up at him. "Thanks, Brack. You're funny for a warlock."

That set both him and Lark off again. It was cute to see the witch and warlock hold each other as they laughed. I was so glad Lark had somebody. She had survived so much. The fact that she was no longer alone made everything we had gone through at the Mythic labs worth it. If we could end Chutka once and for all, perhaps I would be able to keep my promise of her safety.

"Come on," Dara told me. "We have combat training to begin."

As we climbed up the stairs from the basement, her finger slid across the name written on my wrist. A pang of sadness filled me. I hadn't forgotten Sparrow. In fact, the little dragon was never far from my mind. I caught myself searching everywhere I walked in the Academy. I had spent nearly an hour before dinner checking through each plant in Professor Seedly's classroom for any sign of the little dragon even though the professor had told me he hadn't seen her.

"She'll come back when she's ready," the tall, thin professor had reassured me. He ran a hand through his crazy white hair, upsetting the birds in the nest on top. "She's just spreading her wings both figuratively and literally."

"But what if she's in trouble?" I had argued. "How am I supposed to save her if I don't know where she is?"

The professor didn't appear at all concerned by my tone of frustration. Instead, he had replied, "Mr. Briscoe, did you ever consider the fact that perhaps she decided it was time to be on her own? Sylph dragons mature very quickly. Maybe she's ready to find her own kind."

I couldn't help the pathetically lost tone to my voice when I replied, "But I thought you said there weren't any more sylph dragons in the world."

He clucked his tongue and replied. "I didn't say there weren't any more, I said there were very few." He had winked then and gestured to the plant I had accidentally helped to name. "Take it from Gerald. She's safe somewhere in this crazy world, and she'll return if she wants to."

The thought of her not returning made tears burn in my eyes as I followed Dara up the stairs. Maybe the dragon wasn't a baby anymore, but she was tiny and the world outside of the Academy was huge. It may have been safer out there given the fact that we were going to try to summon Chutka the Shambler, but I still hated the thought of Sparrow alone in the world. Maybe she didn't need me, but a big part of me needed to protect her. She was a part of my pack, and I would do everything I could to keep her safe. But she had to be here for me to ensure her safety.

When we reached the main floor and slipped from behind the unicorn painting, the sound of commotion from the cafeteria sent me running.

"What's going on?" Dara asked.

We both stopped in the cafeteria doorway and stared in shock at the scene.

Werewolves, vampires, warlocks, witches, students with orange scales, cat eyes, feathers, or tentacles stood on tables and crouched under them as food flew through the air. Laughter, yelling, and jeering filled the room. A glance at the door to the kitchen showed Mr. Handsworth standing with all four of his hand-tipped tentacles on his hips as he glared at the scene. Spaghetti rested on his bald head and a spattering of broccoli cheese soup colored his white apron. A chuckle nearly escaped me before his eyes locked on mine. The anger in his gaze smothered my mirth completely.

I saw something fly at me from the corner of my eye. I caught a chicken leg before it smacked into my face. The laughter faded as everyone looked at us. Something in my expression must have told them I was serious, because students began to climb down from the tables and out from underneath them.

"What happened here, Rhett?" I demanded when I spotted the werewolves around the tables in the corner.

The werewolf lowered his gaze. "We, uh, thought it would be fun to have a food fight seeing as how we've never had one before."

As much as I couldn't argue with that, my want to laugh or join in was kept in check by Mr. Handsworth's continued glower. Dara didn't appear to care because she laughed anyway.

"Have you gotten it out of your system?" I asked the werewolf.

Rhett glanced around at the other werewolves. They nodded quickly.

"We have," Rhett replied.

I swept my gaze over the rest of the cafeteria and lifted my voice. "Have the rest of you gotten it out of your system?"

I don't know what had turned my position at the Academy from a lone werewolf sitting with an ostracized Grim at a table against the wall to a leader the students apparently respected. I had a sneaking suspicion Alden had been telling stories of our escapades again, because a hint of fear showed in the faces of the students who looked to me as if the food littering their clothes, heads, and, in some cases, multiple faces, was forgotten. Every student nodded.

"Good," I said. "Now, Mr. Handsworth and his staff were kind enough to provide this food for your little battle. Please show your appreciation to him by cleaning the cafeteria and the kitchen from top to bottom."

"Yes, sir," Rhett said.

A series of similar statements followed from the other students.

I didn't like the title, but that moment wasn't the one in which to correct him. The Headmistress would soon be addressing the students about their expected roll in what was to come. I was anxious to get started with my part of it, so I took the initiative.

"Everyone here is in danger." Dara gave me a surprised look, but I crossed my arms in front of my chest and continued with, "You have no doubt heard of some of our battles against demons." I glanced behind me and saw that my team had come to see what all the commotion was about. Alden's cheeks turned red at my searching look, answering my unspoken question. I looked back at the students. "Our biggest battle is soon to begin, and you will all be involved if you so choose."

"I'll fight beside you," Rhett said without hesitation.

"Me, too," another werewolf yelled.

"And me," a vampire joined in.

I lifted a hand before anyone else could get caught up in the enthusiasm. "I appreciate it." I looked back at my team. "We all do. We can use all the help we can get, but it will still be dangerous. My team and I have fought hard to ensure that Haunted High is a safe place for each of you to learn; now we're asking that you join with us in doing the same."

Worry showed in several faces. I looked from one student to the next. "But we won't be throwing you into the fight unprepared. For the next several days, your studies will be taken over by training of a different kind. Those of you with magic affinities will be tutored by Lyris Welkin and Brack Smalls. The rest of you will join us for demon combat training." I smiled at one of the smallest werewolves who had come with me from the Den. "But don't worry. You won't be asked to act beyond your abilities. We have a place for each of you and will strive our best to ensure that you are safe and feel as prepared as we can help you to be." The little werewolf nodded.

I gestured to the students behind me, making plans as I spoke. I hoped I wasn't going beyond the Headmistress' allowance, but since the scope of an assistant professor hadn't been exactly outlined, I took liberties where I wished and chose to suffer the consequences later.

"We'll divide you up by your heritage so that you can be trained by those who know your strengths as well as your weaknesses. Trust your leaders, but don't be afraid to ask questions. And if you feel lost, come find me. We'll make sure you have a place where you fit in."

"When do we start?" Rhett asked.

The expectancy in the air was charged with excitement. I decided to take advantage of that. "As soon as this cafeteria is spotless to Mr. Handsworth's standards." I glanced at the cook and he gave me a nod of approval. "We'll begin training tonight. Werewolves to the forest with me. The rest of you will find your respective tutors from my team and join them where they request. But for now, get to work!" Laughter followed my barked command and the students quickly took the towels Mr. Handsworth gave out and began to clean.

"We're starting their training tonight?" Lorne said in surprise. "What are we supposed to do?"

"Vampire things," I replied. "Fighting, arguing, drinking blood, strangling people you don't want to talk to."

My attempt at a joke fell flat.

Lorne and Jean exchanged glances. "Vicken was our leader. We don't know what we're doing. We're not exactly teachers here."

Lyris and Dara both nodded.

"I hate other people, you know that," Dara said.

"Yeah, Finn," Lyris agreed. "We're winging it."

I motioned for my group to move away from the cafeteria door even though the chaos of cleaning beyond ensured that nobody could overhear us. When we were out of sight from the other students, I leaned against the wall.

"I'm winging it, too," I admitted. "I don't know how to be a leader."

"Right," Brack said. He was as solemn as I had ever seen him. "Alphas are born knowing how to lead."

I stared at him. "You're kidding right?" I looked at each of them. "Do you know how many mistakes I've made? I've nearly gotten you guys killed way too many times!"

Alden grinned. "Well, that's true."

I shook my head. "I'm worse at this than any of you." I met Dara's gaze. "I run toward trouble. Vicken's always getting mad at me for it. You know that."

"But you're brave," Lyris said.

"Or stupid," I reminded her.

"Finn," Dara began.

I shoved my hands in my pockets. "I not saying this to be hard on myself. Trust me. I deserve that. But what I'm saying is that no one is born a leader, at least as far as I know. Even Professor Briggs became a teacher out of circumstance. He wasn't any more ready than we are. Yet look what we've learned!"

"To fear him?" Alden put in helpfully.

I chuckled, thinking that Briggs would like that response. "Yes, and to listen to him. He needs us to respect him in order for us to learn from him."

"How are we supposed to get other students to respect us?" Alden asked. He shoved his white hair out of his eyes. "I can't even get them to pass me the ketchup at lunch."

I smiled at the thought that he was joking, but the seriousness in his light blue eyes made my smile disappear.

"You're right," I realized aloud. "There's only one way to get them to respect any of us. We can tell them stories, but there's no reason for them to believe any of it unless we show them."

"What are you thinking?" Dara asked warily.

I shrugged. "If we want to teach them how to fight demons, we need to show them we know what we're talking about."

"I don't like the sound of that," Lyris said.

Lark's eyes lit up. "I know where some demons are!"

I nodded. "Me, too. Think Headmistress Wrengold will approve a fieldtrip?"

The answer was no, of course. There was no way we could get hundreds of monster students to the worst part of the city.

"There's demons closer to the school," Alden said in a voice that told of how much he hated the idea of returning to the demon world beneath the cemetery.

"But how do we get in without Mezania?" Dara asked.

"We don't," I replied. "There's too many demons down there. We don't want to endanger students needlessly."

Silence fell over the corridor. I couldn't blame my team for their reluctance in training students who might not respect what they had been through. There had to be some way to let the students see that we knew what we were doing without putting anyone in danger. I, for one, wanted to avoid as many encounters with demons as possible, but that went against what my team needed.

"What if you show them?" Dara said.

Her suggestion took me by surprise. "You mean memories?" I asked.

She nodded. "Like you did when you were trying to get Professor Briggs and the others not to kill Conrad. Show the students how we fought the demons, the Wiccan Enforcer, the Demon Knight, and the Darkest Warlock. They'll have to believe us then."

"It won't be just stories," Alden said excitedly.

"I don't know if I can push that hard," I admitted. I looked at Dara. "Even with your help, sharing memories with the professors was difficult. How do we show all the students?"

"You do it with our help."

I turned to see Rhett watching us from the doorway to the cafeteria. The other werewolves crowded behind him.

"We know we made a mess," Rhett apologized. "Maybe we can help make up for it."

"How would you help me share a memory with everyone?" I asked in confusion.

Rhett grinned. "You really aren't good at being a werewolf, are you?"

I laughed. "Not at all. Maybe I needed to spend more time at the Den."

"Definitely not," Rhett replied, his dark eyes glittering. "You got us away from there just in time." He crossed to me; the other werewolves followed. Other monster students began filing out of the cafeteria. Scents of cleaners, lemon, and a lingering hint of spaghetti colored the air.

"There's just one question," Rhett said.

"What's that?" I asked warily.

"Can an old Alpha learn new tricks?"

I grinned. "I'm not that old."

He held out his hand so that it hovered just in front of mine. "This is a trick werewolves learn by the time we're toddlers. It's how we have conversations without our parents being involved." His eyes held sorrow at the loss of his father. "I guess you could say it was our own way of rebelling, only we didn't know it at the time. Now push something at me."

I sent him the memory of us fighting the Demon Knight in the basement. Details like jumping through demon fire, using Mercer's imitation flames to protect my team, and borrowing Dara's strength to grip the key on the Demon Knight's chest came back full force. I was there again, forcing my mind to remain calm while Lyris and Brack chanted, willing my grasp on the key to be sure despite the pain of the fire, and taking a chance to protect the students who didn't know of the doom beneath the school.

When I pulled away, my fingers shook from the force of the memory. I leaned against the wall with my gaze on Rhett.

"That looked like a rough night," he commented, his eyes wide.

I forced a smile. "It gets better."

"I can hardly wait," he replied wryly.

He turned to the next werewolf, a girl named Star who had already made several friends among the monsters.

"I'm going to share with Star and as many students as I can push to," Rhett told me. "Then she'll share with another werewolf who will do the same. We can easily reach everyone in here."

"I can give you strength to reach more," Dara offered.

Rhett shook his head. "Given the memory your boyfriend just showed me, you deserve a break. He wouldn't be here without you, and we wouldn't be here without him. We owe you."

Dara shot me an embarrassed smile as Rhett turned to the other students.

"Close your eyes," he told them. "Clear your minds. I'm going to show you how our Alpha saved your lives."

Chapter Ten

BY THE TIME RHETT and the other werewolves finished sharing the memories of my team defeating each of Chutka's subordinates, along with our run to Lark's basement to trap demons, and the vanquishing of the Darkest Warlock at the Maes headquarters, I felt exhausted. I couldn't avoid the looks of awe mixed with horror on the faces of the students who looked at me. Even my own team had amazed expressions.

"I told you about the Darkest Warlock," I said to Alden in an effort to wipe the hero-worshipping look from his eyes.

"I know," he replied breathlessly, "But it's not the same as seeing it! You should tell us all of your stories that way!"

I glanced at the other students, then looked away from their stunned expressions and said quietly, "I don't think so. I think showing them was a bad idea."

"Why?" Alden replied. "You didn't expose them to danger, and now they have to believe what you guys have been through. It was a great idea!"

I glanced at Dara. The hint of a smile ghosted around her lips as if she found humor in the new adoration I was receiving.

"Stop laughing," I told her.

"I'm not," she replied as her mouth split into a grin. "I'm admiring your bravery."

I fought back a growl of frustration and faced the students. "Let's call it a night."

"Now?" a vampire called out. "But after seeing all of that, I'm ready to learn how to fight demons!"

"Yeah," Adalia from Mrs. Mellon's class said. "You guys defended us. It's our turn. We're not going to cry in a corner while some demon lord tries to take over our school."

"Demon Prince," Dara corrected.

"And he's trying to take over the world, not just Haunted High," Lark put in helpfully.

"All the more reason to start training," Rhett concluded. "We're with you."

I couldn't deny the excitement in the gazes around me. My team had asked for me to help them gain the students' trust. With the expressions on the faces that looked up to us, the team would have no problem getting the monsters to follow what they said.

"Fine," I gave in. "Let the training begin."

A cheer went up from the students. My team began to divide the monsters into groups the way we had decided.

I caught a glimpse of Professor Briggs standing near the unicorn photograph that hid the entrance to the basement and walked over to him.

"I, uh, meant to give them a pep talk in the cafeteria, and it sort of got out of hand," I said.

The professor nodded. "I noticed." He glanced at me. "And I saw the memories."

I lowered my gaze. "I didn't mean for you to."

Professor Briggs watched the students for a moment before he said, "You've been through a lot, Finn."

"We all have," I replied quietly with my gaze on my team. "I couldn't have done it without them."

I saw him nod out of the corner of my eye.

He turned to me. "You're going to make a fine professor someday, Finn."

I stared at him, then realized he was holding out his hand. I shook it. "Thank you, Professor Briggs."

He smiled. "I'll be happy to teach beside you."

I grinned. "Think I have a shot of making them scared of me the way they are of you so they stop looking at me like that?"

He actually laughed. "Not a chance."

I sighed and began to walk back to the werewolves who waited for me.

"Oh, and Finn?" Briggs called out.

I glanced back at him.

He tossed something at me. "This should help!"

I caught the object out of the air, then opened my hand to see a moonstone resting on my palm.

I glared at the professor. He had an actual grin on his face.

"I hate you!" I managed to get out before the phase took over.

My shirt ripped. I made a mental note to tell Briggs he owed me for that one. Luckily, we were in the Academy so I would be able to find my shoes again. With as many shoes as I had lost phasing, I was going to be barefoot before my first year at Haunted High was over.

When I was done phasing, Professor Briggs walked over with a jovial expression and scooped up the moonstone into an ironwood box. I growled at him.

He chuckled. "No hard feelings, Finn, but that's for bringing your uncle back. I know we need his help defeating Chutka and I'll be civil." He winked. "Now."

He pocketed the stone and walked away, leaving the werewolves caught between staring at our little exchange and pretending they didn't notice it.

Rhett cleared his throat. "Well, you see our Alpha. Phase, boys and girls!"

I didn't exactly plan on the corridor being filled with twenty-five werewolves, but it happened. It felt like so much more than just the students who had been milling around. At least I had to give the werewolves credit. They were quiet and controlled as they waited for my orders. The problem was that I didn't know how to give them.

I knew I could push what I wanted done and compel them to follow, but that didn't feel right. Instead, I made my way down the hallway of doors and left them to follow. My fear that the door to the forest would be locked didn't come true. When I approached, the door swung open as if of its own accord.

I was used to such things happening at the Academy, but this time it seemed like too much of a coincidence. I stopped and stared at the door for several long seconds. Things at Haunted High happened in a way that made the school live up to its student-given name. I had taken it for granted on several instances, like the front door opening, as well as the front gate, and the fact that the door to the forest was usually open when I needed it to be. But it suddenly bothered me. Why was it open? Who opened it? Was someone watching me? If so, why didn't I smell them or see them?

With the number of werewolves behind me and the forest beckoning me into the snow with its tantalizing, crisp scent, I pushed my troubled thoughts to the back of my mind. But I vowed to revisit them when I was in human form and such reasoning was easier. There had to be a source behind the assistance I received; I just needed to find out what it was.

When I stepped into the snow, all thoughts of haunted schools, demons, or moonstones left me. Instead came the excited barks and howls of the wolves at my back. I glanced behind me and couldn't help the wolfish grin that spread across my face.

The wolves acted like puppies experiencing their first snow. They snapped at snow mounds, rolled in the fluffy white stuff, and bit at branches that then made the snow tumble off onto their friends. The sight of even the older wolves letting go of their inhibitions to enjoy just being an animal for the moment filled me with joy. Given the way of life I had seen at the Den, I doubted any of them had ever felt so carefree. No matter what, if I failed at everything else, I had given twenty-four werewolves the opportunity to feel happiness and freedom. That was worth celebrating.

I took off through the snow. At a single yip from me, every wolf followed close behind. I ran for the joy of it and to see what the werewolves would do in a wild setting. As I watched, they instinctively branched off in groups of five or six, choosing the weakest to set their pace while the strongest followed at the back to ensure nobody was left behind. It was interesting to watch the pack dynamics. The older wolves watched over the younger ones and helped them navigate the bigger windfalls or streams we crossed.

I chose specific obstacles to see what they would do. Usually, the younger werewolves would watch the way I did it and then attempt to follow. This happened with climbing snow-covered boulders or traveling down ravines. If the younger wolves couldn't make it, the older ones found a safer way around. When we all met up on the other side of the obstacle, every wolf appeared pleased to be a part of the pack.

I began to experiment with compelling the wolves to go where I wanted them. At one point, with a single push of an idea, I ran down the middle of a ravine and directed two groups of five to run on either side at the top. The other wolves followed me to the bottom. With my ears, I kept track of the wolves running above. When the ravine ended and the wolves with me took the trail to the top, we met up with the others who appeared thrilled at following my command.

I chose harder and harder obstacles. At one point, I even sent the werewolves an image of a werewolf in a tree. It was hilarious to see several of the older ones try. The younger werewolves sat around me barking and encouraging their packmates. Snorts of laughter and poofs of snow heralded failed attempts. After the last werewolf fell from the skinny branches, they all turned to me with eager expressions.

The realization of what they expected came with the understanding that a leader should never ask those who follow him or her to do something that the leader wouldn't do. Grinning at my own foolish suggestion, I stood at the base of the tree and studied the branches. It wasn't that they were high up. A good leap would land me on several limbs thicker than my forearm. It was the concept of landing with four feet instead of two and balancing that way.

I had gotten myself into the situation by throwing out what appeared to be an impossible command. It was my turn to try it.

Gathering my paws beneath me, I leaped into the branches. A mad scramble ensued in which I desperately attempted to place all four feet on separate branches. I failed miserably and ended up falling into the snow. The werewolves massed around me with good-natured snorts and huffs of laughter that I returned. I had learned my lesson.

Conscious of the late hour and the fact that the werewolves would all be sleeping in new rooms that night, I turned us back toward the Academy. A single thought from me was enough to disband the control and set the young wolves running after the older ones. Quick games of tag, steal the stick, and other not-so-very leader-like competitions ensued in which I was usually the instigator.

I blamed it on the fact that I had never actually played like a wolf and had apparently missed a very enjoyable part of a werewolf's childhood. I had no problem making up for lost time when it meant solidifying friendships among the wolves and increasing their trust in the strange werewolf who had so drastically altered their entire lives.

A stray scent was enough for me to bark out a command that brought every werewolf back to formation. This time, instead of branching off into separate packs with the weaker members in front, I compelled them fall in behind me. It took only a thought for them to group the younger werewolves in the middle and send the strong wolves to either side and the back. When everyone was set, I advanced forward a step at a time.

My straining senses picked up additional signs of the creatures. The crackling of berry bushes joined with huffing, snuffling sounds. The musky scent that wafted to me said that there were four of them. Each individual smell was unique, but carried similar markers.

At my quiet bark, the werewolves behind me stopped. I advanced alone. Rhett gave a worried whine, but I was glad he didn't follow.

The first bear lifted his head. It was easy to tell by his scent that he was indeed a he, something I hadn't noticed during our rushed introduction at the Den. Gender hadn't seemed important at all during that tense time. But in wolf form, it was easy to tell with a sniff that two of the other bears were female, and the smallest one was a male like the first. My brain catalogued the scents without me thinking about it.

At the biggest bear's huff, the other three bears turned to look at me. I realized how much bigger they were when I was in wolf form. It occurred to me that approaching them as a wolf was probably not the best idea. The bears hadn't exactly been happy about their transportation in the back of the moving truck, but when we reached the Academy and I showed them the path to the forest door, they had run through without hesitation.

It was neat to see them in their natural habitat. The fact that they had found the berry bushes Professor Seedly loved made me wonder how upset he was going to be, but the bears definitely needed it more. They had torn through the beef sides Mr. Handsworth had been generous to provide from the kitchen stock. They also relished the strawberries that Mrs. Mellon donated to the cause. The fact that the professors had turned out so generously after we had told them the reason we had allowed bears to run through the Academy had touched me deeply.

The biggest bear took a few shuffling steps forward. The massive pawprints he left in the snow were as big as my head. I hoped he didn't miss his main sustenance of werewolves from the Den.

I could have compelled him. Pushing the Alpha command would have guaranteed my safety; but it felt wrong. Instead, I waited with my muscles tense and my heart thundering in my chest as the bear drew near. I would run away and compel if I had to, but for the moment I hid my fear that he would smash me flat before realizing I was the one who had saved their lives.

The bear paused about a foot from me. He leaned his snout forward and watched me with his small eyes. His nose touched my forehead and he breathed deeply. When he snorted out, his breath moved my fur. He drew his snout back and watched me down his nose. It was an unsettling moment, me uncertain if I needed to spring away to avoid death, and the bear with his unreadable eyes.

Finally, the animal gave another snort. He pushed his muzzle forward again and bumped his forehead against the side of my face. I grinned and licked his nose by way of what I hoped was a wolf greeting. The bear ambled back to his friends. When he returned to eating the berries, I padded back to the wolves. I hoped the fact that I had narrowly escaped death through my own stupidity didn't show on my face.

Something must have, because Rhett gave a wolfish grin and shoved my shoulder with his. I huffed with laughter and led the werewolves back to the Academy.

"I thought that bear was going to eat you alive!" Rhett said with a laugh when we had phased back to human form.

We sat at the tables in the dark cafeteria going over our little adventure.

"Yeah," a werewolf named Lizzy said. "He was, like, fifty times bigger than you! How did you dare to approach him?"

"He's the Alpha," a young boy who went by Gimmick told them. The awe on the boy's face when he looked at me made me feel uncomfortable. "He can do anything!"

"Well, not anything," I told him. "But I have the bad habit of trying anyway."

The other werewolves laughed.

It felt nice to sit there after the run. The camaraderie with the werewolves was unmistakable.

"It was awesome running and knowing exactly where you wanted us to go," a boy close to my age said. "I've never felt that before. It was as though each of us fit into some sort of machine, and every piece had a purpose."

I nodded. "It felt that way for me, too." I smiled at the eager group. "This is honestly my first time being in a wolf pack." I gestured at the Academy. "I've been alone at Haunted High since I started."

"Why weren't werewolves allowed here?" a girl asked.

They deserved to know the truth. They might not have to face as much prejudice as I did, but it was vital that they know the danger one of their kind had brought to the Academy, and why parents wouldn't be thrilled that more werewolves had been allowed back.

"You know what I showed you about the demons?" The mood became solemn as each of the werewolves nodded. "Well, it was a werewolf who released the demons in the first place. He was tricked, he wanted power, and one of the demons used that to control him and attack students and professors at this school." Sorrow and horror showed on the faces around me. It echoed the emotions in my heart. "A lot of people were killed. Some students even had to become professors to keep the Academy running. It was a hard time for them, and it took a long time for the other monsters to learn to trust werewolves again." I gave a wry smile. "They're still learning. We just have to be patient. Fighting Chutka is going to go a long way in dealing with that. We have to stay strong, stick together, and always act for the good of the pack. Can you do that for me?"

Nods came from every student.

That brought another smile to my face. "I know you can. I feel how happy you are to be here. I know you're going to enjoy it when the demons are gone and our schedules return to normal. This is a great place; you'll see."

A little girl raised her hand.

"Yes, Misty?" I asked.

"Some of the monsters are scary," she said in a timid voice.

I nodded with a warm smile. “They are, but you know what?” I said, leaning forward.

“What?” she asked.

“Every monster in here is my friend,” I told her. I might have been stretching the truth a bit, but I figured that was alright. I hadn’t had a class with every monster at the Academy, but my goal was for the prejudice against werewolves to be completely gone by the end of the year; viewing each student as a friend helped me treat them that way. If I could get the other werewolves to do the same, we might have a chance of succeeding. “Every student at the Academy wants to learn and grow just the way you do,” I said. “And they each have families that love them, and friends they like to hang out with.” I winked at her. “I’ll bet if you give them a chance, they’ll want you to be their friend, too.”

Her eyes were wide when she asked, “But what if they don’t?”

“Then you come talk to me,” I told her. “I find out what the problem is and we’ll fix it together, okay?”

That made her smile. “Okay, Mr. Alpha, Sir.”

I laughed. “Call me Finn.” I looked around at the rest of the group. “Everyone, please call me Finn. I’m not a very good Sir, and I’m still learning how to be an Alpha. Finn suits me fine and I’ll even answer to it.”

The older werewolves chuckled. Gimmick rubbed his eyes.

I stood up. “Time for all good werewolves to get to bed. You each have your bunkmates, right?” The youngest ones nodded while the older ones shepherded them closer. I couldn’t help the pride that filled me when I looked at them. “I’m so glad you’re here,” I told them honestly. “The Academy needs you and I need you. We’re going to make an awesome pack, I promise. Now get some sleep.”

“Goodnight, Mr. Alpha Finn, Sir,” Misty said sleepily as she followed Star to the stairs.

A chuckle escaped me as I watched them go.

Rhett waved before helping Gimmick up the stairs toward the room they would share. I waved back and then leaned against the doorframe to the cafeteria as I watched them file tiredly away.

"You're going to make an awesome pack, huh?" a voice said from behind me.

Chapter Eleven

I SPUN AROUND TO see Uncle Conrad watching me. I wasn't sure when he had entered the cafeteria, but the sight of him standing there with his hands in his pockets made me sad. He had eaten in this same cafeteria as a student, and probably laughed and joked the way my new werewolf pack did. I didn't have to wonder if he missed it. The answer was there in his eyes that matched my mom's.

"How many werewolves were here before?" I asked quietly.

"Eleven," he replied. He lifted a shoulder. "I guess you could say it was a slow couple of years for werewolves."

I asked the question I didn't want to. "How many—"

"All of them besides your mother," he answered without waiting for me to finish. His head hung low. "I killed all of them, Finn. I watched the Darkest Warlock tear through their bodies with my hands and leave them there to die. And I couldn't stop him."

He looked at me, his gaze haunted. "I hear them here, laughing and running through the halls, howling to scare the other students like we used to, chasing each other and seeing who could phase the fastest." He looked around him, his gaze distant. "I'm surrounded by the ghosts of the people I love most, and it's all my fault they're not here."

I thought of Vicken's words to my uncle. "You didn't know what you were doing or who you were freeing."

My uncle fell silent with a lost expression on his face. I wanted to help him, but I didn't know what to say. I wished Dara was there to ease his pain, but she didn't deserve it, either. Her ability was both a blessing and a curse. I didn't want her to hurt in order to help others who were haunted by their own actions.

A thought occurred to me. I glanced at the werewolf. "Uncle Conrad?"

"You don't have to call me that. I haven't exactly been much of an uncle to you," he replied morosely without looking at me.

I gave him a small smile. "You saved my life. That's pretty uncle-like if you ask me."

He glanced at me. The barest ghost of a smile touched his eyes but not his mouth. "I guess it is."

I nodded. "So, Uncle Conrad, do you know why this place is called Haunted High?"

He gave me a skeptical look as if he thought I was playing a joke on him. "The ghosts. Trace told me you encountered a few of those. Sounds like it was a bit of a nightmare."

I nodded. "Yes, but what I'm asking is different. Is there something else to this place? Some sort of spirit or something that makes it alive?"

He watched me closely. "Why do you ask?"

I lifted a shoulder. "Well, I don't really know how to put it." I didn't want my uncle to think I was completely crazy. By his expression, he was nearly there. I sighed and told the truth. "Ever since I came here, things have been happening, things I can't account for."

"Like what?" he asked.

I cleared my throat in embarrassment and said, "Well, doors open when I need them to, the gate lets me in and out sometimes, and once, I heard a whisper. It was actually the first day I got here."

Uncle Conrad's expression was unreadable when he said, "What did it say?"

"It said, 'Welcome to Haunted High.'" I remembered the way air had brushed across the back of my neck as though someone was breathing there, but when I had turned around, I was alone. "It's just, well, unsettling."

A true smile warmed my uncle's face. "Then you've met Cadish."

"Who's Cadish?" I asked.

"Your mother's imaginary friend," Uncle Conrad replied.

I couldn't help staring at him. "What do you mean, my mother's imaginary friend?"

"Silvia had a great imagination." Uncle Conrad's smile took on a wistful look. "I wish you knew her when she was your age. She was all spunk and pep. When she laughed, the whole room would join in." He shook his head. "I was the older one, but I always found myself following her around. It was like she held some sort of magic over us. She used to tell us stories, and most of those included her imaginary friend, Cadish."

His words didn't make any sense. As much as I loved hearing him talk about my mother, her stories and what I had experienced didn't coincide. "But if he was imaginary, why do things happen as if he's real?"

"Because she made him real," Conrad explained.

I sighed. "Now you're the one telling a story.

Conrad smiled and motioned for me to join him at a table. I sat down across from him and leaned my elbows on the top.

"Your mother was stubborn. I see the same stubbornness in you," he said. "When she wanted something to happen, no amount of persuasion would change her mind." His gaze took on a distant cast. "When she was about ten, she decided that she'd told enough stories about Cadish. It was time that he was able to experience them with us." He shrugged. "I guess she figured he was real enough to her that he should be real to everyone."

"How is that even possible?" I asked.

Uncle Conrad opened a hand. "Well, when you're friends with witches and warlocks, strange things can happen." He winked. "Especially when there's a Grim involved."

The thought of my mother being friends with a Grim like I was made me smile. I had to admit that strange things happened with my friends. Maybe it wasn't so farfetched to believe the same occurred with my mother.

"So they made Cadish?" I guessed.

He shook his head. "More like they gave life to her stories of him, only it didn't happen the way she wanted." He pointed to a corner of the cafeteria. "In fact, it happened right over there. I remember her plans. She had read every spell in the library and even stolen, or borrowed," he corrected with a wink, "A few books from Professor Frogson. In the books, she found a way to make her imagination come to life. Her friends were more than willing to participate, and she dragged me along as a mostly unwilling spectator." He sighed. "I was always afraid when Silvia got that look in her eye."

I fought back a smile at the fact that Alden and Vicken had occasionally said the same thing about me.

"So what happened?" I pressed, intrigued.

Uncle Conrad looked at the corner of the cafeteria as if he saw the scene unfold again. "The witches and warlocks recited the spell she found as she told her favorite stories about him, and your mother used moonstones to turn her memories into a soul." He shook his head. "From what I've heard, that's not supposed to happen. But your mother was something special, and I think she hoped so much that it just had to work."

"So Cadish became real?"

Uncle Conrad nodded. "In a sense. I actually saw him for a moment. The air shimmered, a figure formed in the circle, and the real life Cadish smiled at your mother. She laughed her contagious laugh and said, 'Hi, Cadish!' as if she wasn't even surprised to see him. The rest of us were staring like idiots." He chuckled. "I think one of the warlocks actually passed out from shock." His smile fell. "And then it happened."

"What happened?" I asked.

"One of the moonstones broke." He opened his hand. "It shattered, the circle cracked, and then Cadish disappeared." He shook his head. "Silvia was heartbroken. We tried to get him back, but nothing we did made a difference. We even found another moonstone and redid the ceremony, but we couldn't get him to appear again."

I felt sad even though I hadn't been there. The thought of my mother's friend vanishing was heartbreaking when I imagined how she must have felt.

"But Silvia told me months later that Cadish wasn't gone," Conrad continued with wonder in his voice. "She said he simply wasn't like us. She told me he helped her sometimes, like a guardian angel. He watched over her. She said it was his way of showing how grateful he was to have a soul." Uncle Conrad looked at me. "I think that's who's helping you. Maybe Cadish knows you're your mother's son."

"Maybe," I replied. The thought was comforting.

Running footsteps sounded from the corridor. I was standing before I even realized I had moved. When Dara appeared, my muscles were tense and I had to fight back the urge to phase and protect her from whatever had made her so desperate to find me.

"What is it?" I asked, hurrying to her.

"Demons," she said, gasping for air. "The basement is full of them!"

I looked at Uncle Conrad.

"Where are the heart pieces?" he asked. "We have to act, now!"

"The Headmistress has them in her office; but we're not ready!" I told him.

"We have to be ready," he replied. "Get the team. Chutka knows we're up to something. If we don't bind the heart to the moonstone now, we won't have a chance against him."

Dara and I ran up the stairs. I stopped to get Alden while Dara continued up after the others.

I burst into the room we shared. "Alden, wake up!" I shouted.

The Grim sat up and groggily rubbed his eyes. "What's going on?"

"Demons are coming for the heart pieces. If we don't perform the spell now, everything will be lost," I quickly explained.

Alden jumped out of bed. "Where's the others?"

"Dara's waking the team up. The students aren't ready," I said.

"We need them anyway," the Grim replied. "Wake them up."

"All of them? How?" I asked, surprised at his commanding tone.

"Howl, Finn. Summon your pack. You're a werewolf. Put that to use."

I stared at him. "Alden, you're a genius."

He grinned and pushed his mussed hair out of his face. "I'm glad somebody noticed."

I ran to the door and cupped my hands around my mouth. I sucked in a deep breath and let out a long, low howl that reverberated up the stairs. It would have been easier to howl as a wolf, but telling the students afterwards would have been impossible. Fortunately, the werewolves responded immediately.

"What's going on?" Rhett asked from further up the stairs the moment my howl stopped. Several other werewolves poked their heads out from behind him.

"The demons are here. We need to act now!" I told them.

Rhett looked behind him. "Round up the rest of the students. Meet Finn in the corridor."

Werewolves took off running.

Out of habit, I reached back to shut the door to our room and saw my cellphone flashing. I picked it up and glanced at the message.

HOW'D THE TRAINING GO? WHEN IS THE SPELL BEING CAST? I CAN HELP.- VICKEN

I wrote back quickly. *THINGS ARE FINE. GET BETTER.- FINN*

I tossed the phone down and ran out of the room. The last thing Vicken needed during his recovery was to worry about our team in trouble. I rushed down the stairs with the thought that at least he and Kiyah would be safe.

Professor Briggs burst through the unicorn painting the moment I reached the corridor. He shoved the picture shut again and leaned against it.

"The demons are coming," he said, his face pale and chest heaving. "We need to perform the ceremony."

"Dara told me." I put my shoulder against the photograph. "The students are coming. Where's the Headmistress?"

"In her office," Briggs replied.

Headmistress Wrengold appeared in the hallway. "I'm right here."

"Where are we going to do this?" I asked.

The Headmistress gestured toward the corridor in which we stood. "Here. We need the room, and it's defendable."

Professors hurried from the hallway. Headmistress Wrengold began giving out orders. "Bamenda, shield the windows."

Mrs. Hassleton lifted her hand and the windows that lined one side of the great corridor immediately darkened.

"Mr. Smalls, seal the doors so the demons don't catch us by surprise," the Headmistress continued.

Brack motioned with one hand. I heard the lock click on the massive front doors followed by the doors in the long hallway.

Other students were beginning to arrive. By the controlled terror on their faces, I guessed that the werewolves had told them what we were up against. Fortunately, no one appeared to be panicking, yet.

Dara ran down the stairs followed by Lyris.

"Let's begin the binding," the Headmistress instructed.

At her motion, Brack grabbed a marble-topped end table and carried it over as though it weighed nothing. Headmistress Wrengold set the three boxes on top. Professor Briggs left me at the picture frame to carry over the one containing the moonstone. The demons scrabbled against the unicorn picture. My feet began to slide backwards despite my werewolf strength.

"Brack, a little help here?" I called out.

The huge warlock looked at me. When he saw my predicament, he lifted a hand. I felt the frame stop moving.

"I've got it," Brack called.

I took a hesitant step backwards. When the picture frame stayed put despite the yowling and protests of the demons beyond, I let out a sigh of relief.

The Headmistress opened the three boxes, revealing the pieces of Chutka's heart.

"Conrad," she instructed as she opened the one with the moonstone. Careful not to touch the stone, the Headmistress tipped the box and let it fall in the middle of the table.

My uncle gave her a worried look. "Are you sure you want me to do this?"

She nodded. "Let's finish what you started."

The fear in Conrad's eyes was unmistakable. "Alright, but once I begin, I won't be able to stop." He swallowed. "Trust me. I tried last time."

His reference to the slaughter that had ensued sent tension through the air.

I had to give the Headmistress credit for how steady her voice was when she said, "Begin."

My uncle sucked in a shaky breath and began to chant in a language I didn't recognize. The darkness of the words sent a chill down my spine. My instincts told me to distance myself from him, but I pushed down the feeling. Instead, I crossed closer to the table as the other students formed their circle. My werewolf pack came up behind me. I could feel their presence without looking at them.

A hand touched my arm. I felt Dara's reassuring presence. "Let's finish this," she said quietly.

I nodded. "It's time."

"Begin the shield," Lyris said at my words.

The students behind us repeated the witch's chant. Brack's deep voice followed along with the other warlocks. The air shimmered and a shield glowed, ready to solidify at my command.

In front of Conrad, the stones began to pulse. Darkness flowed outward from them in a thick, snaking mist. The pieces of Chutka the Shambler's heart vibrated in their open boxes. Dark power surged outward in beckoning waves. I heard Uncle Conrad groan. His hands reached toward the heart pieces. The tendrils of mist snaked down his arms.

"The moonstone," I said.

Conrad ignored me. His gaze was on the black heart pieces. I could see the reflection of the pulsing power in his gaze. My chest tightened at the thought that we were about to see history repeat itself. If Conrad allowed Chutka to take over his body the way the Darkest Warlock had done, there was no way I could stop him. Already, I could feel the Demon Prince's power growing. If he gained a form he could control, we would all be lost.

I closed my eyes, but fear pressed against me. I had seen what Conrad did the first time. Briggs, Headmistress Wrengold, my mother, and so many of the students and professors at the Academy had suffered as a result. I didn't want my friends, my pack, or my team to go through the same thing.

A hand slipped into mine. Before I could question whose it was, my fears faded and calm reassurance filled me. I knew what to do and how I could help. I opened my eyes and shot Dara a grateful look. She nodded.

With a calming breath, I pushed a command at Conrad. "Bind the moonstone."

The werewolf glanced at me. I pushed the command again. "Bind the moonstone, now."

My uncle's eyes widened. He looked from the heart pieces to the moonstone that lay in the middle of the table. Uncle Conrad's jaw clenched. He picked up the first box and turned it over so that the heart piece rolled to a stop beside the moonstone. He tossed the ironwood box to the floor. Sweat beaded on his forehead as he did the same to the second and then the third boxes.

"Begin the spell," the Headmistress said.

On her command, the professors around her read from the pieces of paper they held. The mythics in charge of Haunted High began the spell tentatively. They hadn't had much time to practice; I was impressed they had found the spell in the first place. Fortunately, as they read, their recitation became stronger. With Professor Mellon's clear voice leading the group, the professors repeated the spell over and over in time to the chants Lyris and Brack lead.

The heart pieces drew closer to the moonstone as though it was a magnet. The darkness that snaked through the air circled the moonstone but didn't touch it. I watched breathlessly as the stones first touched and then enveloped the moonstone. The mist circled faster. Uncle Conrad's dark words became a crude counterbalance to the lyrical chants that flowed around the room. The darkness of the stones intensified, first shrouding the moonstone and then cutting off its light entirely.

The moment the pieces joined to form a complete circle, a giant crack appeared in front of Conrad. It looked as though a knife had been drawn across the air on the other side of the table. Gasps sounded through the corridor when a huge, pale, clawed hand reached through. A second hand appeared. The claws grabbed the edges of the crack. A tearing sound followed as the claws forced the crack wider. Students held their ears and others cried at the echoing, screeching noise. It felt as though the sound came from inside of my head as well as outside.

Horns, another set of clawed hands, and then a snout of needle-like teeth followed.

I could only stare as Chutka the Shambler forced the crack wide open and then stepped into our world.

Massive black hooves bigger than my head met the marble floor in a shower of sparks. My eyes moved up to a long, lashing tail that sliced through the air with the hiss of a whip. Massive, thick black leathery wings dragged against the floor. The Demon Prince wore the darkness around him like a cloak. It writhed and moved as though it was a living creature. Curled horns swept back from a pale forehead that looked as though it had never seen the light of day. Eyes set deep above the dragon-like snout searched the room before landing on my uncle.

A snort of amusement escaped Chutka the Shambler. The Demon Prince straightened up to his full height so that he towered far above Uncle Conrad.

"I didn't think you had it in you to bring me here." Chutka's voice felt like claws inside my ears. "I underestimated your loyalty."

When he chuckled, I reached up and was amazed to find that my ears weren't bleeding.

Chutka's eyes shifted from Uncle Conrad to the students and professors surrounding him.

"Pets, attack," the Demon Prince said casually.

A tearing sound heralded the demons as they burst through the unicorn painting. Students screamed and professors moved to bar their path. The demons' grins showed their anticipation at the slaughter. Green fire bubbled from their jaws and spilled onto the ground. The cries of fear the students gave made the demons even more excited. They surged forward.

A crash sounded from the hall of many doors. I glanced over my shoulder just as a purple and black form streaked past my face, followed by an orange and black one, a yellow and green one, and then a hundred more so fast they were a blur. But my eyes stayed with the black and purple form.

Sparrow fanned her wings backwards just before she reached the first demon. A puff of blue flame spouted from her muzzle toward the creature. When it hit the demon's face, the creature's flame sputtered and went out. The demon yelped and back peddled. Sparrow let out a hiss. The other sylph dragons attacked, swarming the demons like a rush of angry hornets. The demons yelped and scrambled over each other in an effort to get away. The dragons pursued them through the torn photograph. Yowls and cries of pain followed the dragons' flight.

My relief at seeing Sparrow safe vanished at the sound of the Demon Prince's voice.

"Pests," Chutka growled. "Vermin!" He lifted his hands and grew bigger as we watched, towering above all of the students in the room. Around me, students cringed and cowered away from the Demon Prince. Their chanting became sporadic and the shield that protected them faltered.

"The shield!" Alden said before I could tell them. "Don't let it fall!"

At the Grim's command, the students' chants increased, echoing from the ceiling and the walls. The shield between us and Chutka solidified into a golden, iridescent wall.

"I see you found my heart," Chutka said with a toothy grin. He picked up the black lump from the table in front of Conrad. It appeared small in his massive pale hand, but I could feel the dark power that wafted from it. "I should thank you," he continued in his defiling voice. "But I knew you were spineless. You had to finish what you started. That's why I chose you."

"For the power," Uncle Conrad said.

I had to give him credit for keeping his voice steady.

"Yes," Chutka replied with a pleased, terrifying grin. "Your greed is my gain." He looked at those behind Conrad; the students and professors backed up when his gaze met theirs. "And you've brought followers." He nodded. "All in due time. First, this."

He drove one of his claws into his chest. Black blood leaked from the wound as he drew the claw down. Opening the cavity wide, he revealed a dark, throbbing mass. Toward the top, a chunk was missing. The black blood that flowed around the misshapen heart leaked down the sides and spilled into the cavity, coloring the pale skin in a dark, angry bruise.

Chutka shoved the piece he held into the cavity.

"Yes," He breathed with a rumbling groan that made the ceiling shake. "Complete at last."

When he took his hand away, the gaping wound in his chest closed. The skin sealed together as though it had never been torn. The black blood that marred his pale skin lifted into the swirling darkness that surrounded him. Chutka gave a sigh of pleasure as he looked down at Conrad once more.

"My turn." His massive claws reached for my uncle.

Chapter Twelve

"NOW!" I YELLED.

Mrs. Hassleton snapped her fingers and the shielding over the windows vanished. Moonlight streamed onto Chutka's shoulders. His head jerked back and he stared up at the windows in surprise. The place where he had put the missing piece of his heart started to glow. One massive hand grabbed his chest. A grimace of pain rippled across his face.

"No," he snarled. He glared at Conrad. "What have you done?"

Green froth bubbled from the Demon Prince's mouth and down his chest. Before my uncle could react, the froth ignited into green fire.

"You'll pay for this," Chutka growled.

The flames ran down his body to the floor where it spilled hungrily toward my uncle. Conrad's eyes were wide and fear showed in every line of his body, but he made no move to get away.

"Run!" I shouted and pushed toward the werewolf.

Green fire sprang up in front of me, blocking me from reaching him. The flames were repelled by the shield wall Lyris and the other students held fast with their chanting. The glow of the wall intensified with their strength.

Chutka's eyes narrowed as he looked from my uncle to me.

"I know you," he said. Realization dawned on his face. "You're behind this. You're behind all of this!"

"You're finished, Chutka," I shouted past the roar of the flames. "You have no more power here!"

"That's where you're wrong," the Demon Prince replied.

He lifted his hand and the flames surrounded my uncle. Conrad let out a shout of pain.

"No!" I cried.

I shoved my hand through the wall. The green flames licked at my skin. I knew the fire could only hurt me if I gave into my fear. The healed burn across my palm throbbed. Pain shot up my arm. I leaned into the flame, reaching for my uncle. I held back a scream as the fire rushed up my shoulder. I couldn't let it break down my walls. It wouldn't have any power if I kept strong. But the fire was so much hotter than it had been with the regular demons. The Demon Prince would win. I would be covered in scars like Professor Briggs, or worse, burned to a pile of smoldering ash.

Just as my walls began to falter and the pain became real, a hand grabbed my shoulder. The pain diminished enough that I could breathe. I latched onto Uncle Conrad's arm and pulled backwards in an attempt to drag him through the shield.

"He's mine," Chutka growled.

At his motion, the flames rose higher, engulfing both my uncle and me. Conrad let out a bloodcurdling scream. I pulled back in an attempt to draw his pain, but mine was so great I could barely think.

The pain cleared. It was startling enough that I glanced backwards to see what was happening. Rhett had taken Dara's other hand. His eyes were closed and beads of sweat showed on his forehead. Star had his other hand, followed by Gimmick and the others. The entire wolf pack that had come back with me from the Den held hands and shared my pain. Tears broke from my eyes and immediately went up in steam. I pulled backwards, drawing Uncle Conrad with me.

"No!" Chutka yelled.

"You're finished," my uncle said through gritted teeth. His clothes were a mess of soot and ash and his face was twisted in pain. Despite his burns, he began the chant again.

The crack behind Chutka widened. The wound in his chest burst open and light appeared. A grating, harsh howl sounded from the Demon Prince.

"You will pay for this, werewolf scum!" Chutka said, his words thick with pain.

Before I could react, the Demon Prince shoved his claws through Conrad's chest.

"No!" I shouted.

Chutka yanked his claws free and my uncle fell to the floor. Chutka raised his hand to finish the job. I crouched over Conrad in the flames, fully expecting to feel the Demon Prince's claws. Time seemed to slow. My breath rattled in my ears. I heard demons scream in the basement as they battled the sylph dragons. I hoped Sparrow was safe. Students cried out in fear and the sound of someone screaming came above the roar of the green flames that surrounded me. My heart pounded.

I heard Chutka's claws slice through the air. I tensed, expecting to be torn in half. Instead, a form shoved between me and the Demon Prince. I looked up to see Professor Briggs above me. He held his walking stick in both hands. His face twisted at the strain of holding Chutka's huge claws at bay. The wood of the stick began to crack.

"You couldn't protect the girl you loved," Chutka said in a voice that was filled with both pain and mocking laughter. "What makes you think you can protect the boy?"

"I failed once," Briggs replied in a growl. "I won't fail again!"

"You can't stop me!" Chutka said. He lifted his arms, growing larger. "I am too strong for you!"

A black and white form flew past my head. The Headmistress in her night owl form flapped her wings once and surged through the windows above us, shattering them. Moonlight spilled unhindered onto Chutka the Shambler. The hole in the Demon Prince's chest opened wider. He let out a bloodcurdling scream. The crack behind him tore into a massive hole. Chutka grabbed Professor Briggs and shoved him toward the crack. Off-balance, Briggs fell against the hole. He tried to push free, but he was sucked into the darkness.

"Professor!" I shouted.

Chutka the Shambler turned to face me.

"I told you I would destroy everything you care about," he said in a voice that grated through my mind with the pain of a thousand claws.

On the other side of the flames, I saw students cringe at the sound. The flames rose higher. Only the steadying hand on my arm kept me centered.

"I keep my promises," Chutka said.

His massive, clawed hand reached for me. I waited for the feeling of his claws tearing through my body, but it never came. Instead, his hand shot past me and latched onto someone else.

Dara screamed as she was pulled through the flames. Chutka fell backwards into the crack and pulled the empath after him.

"Dara!" I shouted.

Tears filled Dara's eyes when she met my gaze. It was the last thing I saw before the Demon Prince pulled her through to the other side. The flames vanished.

I lunged toward the crack, but a hand caught my shirt in a vice-like grip I knew could only come from one person.

I spun to see Vicken, his face pale and chest heaving as he held onto my shoulder.

"What are you doing?" he demanded.

"I've got to save Dara and Briggs!" I told him. "I can't leave them there to die!"

He shook his head. "You can't go through the crack; you'll never come back!"

"I can't leave them there!" I said. "I won't!"

My eyes shifted from the vampire to Alden. The Grim knelt beside my uncle. When he put his hands on Conrad's chest in an attempt to stop the flow of blood, I saw the name *Conrad Justin Roe* glowing in blue writing on his forearm.

"He won't stop," I said, my voice shaking with rage. "He won't stop until he destroys everything we care about. If we don't finish him, this school, my family, your family, the werewolves, and this entire world will be destroyed by Chutka and his demons. I have to go."

"Hurry!" Lyris called. "We can't hold it open much longer!"

A glance behind me showed the truth of her statement. Every professor, witch, and warlock at Haunted High chanted. Sweat and strain showed on the pale faces.

"We won't be able to open it again from this side!" Brack said. His wide gaze showed his emotions when he continued with, "It's a one-way ticket, Finn. You might not come back."

"Then I'll make sure Chutka can't, either," I vowed.

I looked at Vicken.

"Running toward trouble?" the vampire asked.

"Always," I replied.

He nodded. "Let's go."

He helped me to my feet and we reached the crack together. The moment we stepped through, the world changed. Sound came from inside of me instead of outside. The internal workings of my body, the push of blood through my veins, the rush of breath in and out of my lungs, and even the sound of my muscles, tendons, and joints created a symphony that was familiar and strange at the same time. I blinked and the noise of my eyelids closing and opening sounded like the flap of a pair of wings.

Every sound signified one very important thing. I was alive in a realm of others who were not.

As soon as the thought solidified, sound returned. I wished it hadn't.

Thousands of shrieking, screeching, squealing, and yowling voices pushed against my ears. A noise like a giant piece of tape being torn off cardboard sounded. I looked back to see the last glimmer of moonlight vanish. The crack was sealed. Only a faint ripple in the gray light that surrounded us remained to show where it had been.

"Where to?"

Vicken's voice sounded flat and bizarre. I looked at him. In the dull light, his skin appeared unhealthy and washed out. His yellow eyes were too bright and his teeth glowed faintly. A chill ran down my spine. He truly looked like a monster.

"Your eyes are glowing," he said warily. "You look feral. Are you alright?"

I nodded, shoving my concerns about him aside. He had followed me into the demon realm to save the girl I loved. Now wasn't the time to distrust him. "I think it's this place. It makes my skin prickle. I feel like lightning's about to strike or something."

He nodded and ran his hands over his arms in an unsettled gesture I had never seen from him. "It's creepy. Let's kill Chutka and get out of here as fast as we can."

"Deal," I replied. I gestured in the direction of the demon voices. "I'm guessing we go that way."

Vicken sighed. "It has to be toward the sound of a million painful deaths, doesn't it?"

"Of course," I replied.

Our footsteps thudded dully in my ears. The strange world solidified around us as we walked. Nothing took solid form, but hints of images and forms peeked from the edges of my vision. Outlines of buildings meant that we were on some sort of street. Forms that could have been trees were tipped in spikes instead of leaves. Shorter plants, perhaps flowers once, twisted and writhed as though in pain.

Everywhere I looked, demons ghosted at the edges of my vision. I could feel the presence of hundreds beyond those I could see. As they followed us, their skittering claws and strange spider-like way of walking sent tremors across my skin. There were far more than we had ever faced. Brack's warning of a one-way ticket echoed in my mind.

"I shouldn't have let you follow me here," I said to Vicken.

He glanced at me. "You couldn't have stopped me."

I gave him a frank look. The skin around his eyes tightened and he grimaced slightly with each step. I had no doubt his head wound hadn't healed completely, and the frailty of his form was something I had never seen before.

"I could have." I shook my head. "I told you on the phone that things were fine. You were supposed to stay home and heal."

Vicken rolled his eyes. "You saying things are fine is like someone else waving a red flag and shouting that they're about to dive headfirst into danger. I had to come."

"So you could be the one to dive headfirst into danger?" I pointed out.

Vicken opened his mouth to argue, then shut it again. When he finally spoke, it was to change the subject. "So what's your plan?"

I had to admit that it was a pretty good subject change. Given the enormity of what we were about to face, a plan would definitely be a good idea. I went with what I had so far. "Find Briggs, get Dara way from Chutka, then kill him and find a way back home."

Vicken thought about it for a moment and then nodded. "I suppose that's a start. How do we find—Finn, look!"

I followed his finger and saw bright flashes of color amongst the gray.

"Sparrow!" I shouted.

The whirlwind of sylph dragons turned as one and shot toward us. Just when I was afraid they were going to attack, the purple and black dragon at the lead surged forward and spun around me in a tight circle. Her tiny tongue licked my cheek and she darted around my neck and arms so fast I couldn't help laughing.

"I missed you, too!" I told her.

The tiny dragon landed on my hand. I ran a finger down her neck. When I lifted her up, she rubbed against my chin like a cat.

"I was so worried about you!" I said.

She blinked her bright green eyes as her tail lashed from side to side. Her name written across the base of my left wrist tingled.

"Uh, Finn?"

I looked over to see at least a dozen of the dragons perched on Vicken's shoulders and arms. He appeared terrified to move. An orange and yellow dragon stood on the vampire's hand and was watching him steadily with bright red eyes.

"Making friends?" I asked.

"Hoping not to be eaten," Vicken replied.

That made me smile. "You're a hundred times their size."

"But there's more of them," the vampire pointed out. "They have strength in numbers."

"So do we, now," I said.

Vicken shot me an incredulous look. "You think these puny little dragons are going to give us an advantage against Chutka?"

The dragon on Vicken's hand flicked out its tongue. The vampire winced.

I lifted a shoulder. "I'll take any help we can get." I looked down at Sparrow. "Think you can ask your friends to give Vicken a break? He's scared."

Vicken gave an almost-believable laugh. "I'm not scared. I'm just practical. Vampires and flying rats don't get along."

Sparrow leaped off my hand. The other dragons immediately followed. She blew a small, misty flame at Vicken that vanished before it reached him. He took several wary steps back just the same.

"Flying rats?" I asked as they circled over our heads and proceeded to follow us. "You've just offended an entire species."

Vicken kept his gaze on the dragons as if certain they were about to attack him. "I apologize to rats."

I fought back a laugh. "You and I get along."

"That's circumstantial," Vicken replied.

"And what do you call this?" I asked. "I'll take any allies we can get."

Vicken looked around us. "You have a point."

I was about to revel in the fact that I had actually won an argument against the vampire when a form lunged from the shadows.

"Vicken, look out!" I shouted.

I rushed in front of the vampire and was about to phase when the form straightened. I stopped short at the sight of Professor Briggs.

Blood coated his dark cloak and robes in several places. By the thick smell of it, I knew the professor was badly injured. Despite that, he brandished his cane like a sword and prepared to strike at us.

"Professor Briggs, it's us," I said.

He blinked, looked from me to Vicken, and lowered his cane. "Boys?"

I nodded.

A furrow formed between his eyebrows. "What are you doing here?"

"Saving you," Vicken said. He glanced at me. "And Dara. Do you know where Chutka took her?"

"I followed them as fast as I could, but I couldn't keep up." He put a hand to his chest. I could hear his breath wheezing through his lungs.

"You should wait here," I told him. "We'll come get you when we stop Chutka."

Briggs shook his head. "I won't let you go alone. You can't stop him by yourselves."

"We're not alone," I replied. I gestured.

The professor followed my gaze. A smile touched his lips at the sight of the dragons flying above us. "You brought an army."

I nodded. "Stay here, Professor. We've got this."

He straightened. "I have my own vendetta to settle. Come if you wish, but don't get in my way." He limped forward.

Vicken and I exchanged a glance and hurried after him.

Chapter Thirteen

A BUILDING OF DARK, swirling mist solidified in the distance. As we drew closer, the presence of the demons increased. They became bold enough to trail our footsteps and spit fire at our legs. The sylph dragons answered with red, blue, green, and orange fires of their own, swooping and hissing to send the demons back from the trail. One nearly bit my fingers before Sparrow attacked and sent it yelping into the distance. She settled on my shoulder after that. The familiarity of her tiny claws in my shirt calmed my nerves. Even Vicken didn't appear to mind when the rest of the dragons flew closer to us.

The building turned out to be merely broken, crumbling walls so long they faded into the distance. In the middle was a huge hole instead of a door as though the building had been ripped into by some massive, terrible creature I didn't want to meet.

We followed Briggs inside to find that instead of a ceiling, a swirling canopy of green flames writhed and danced like a bone-melting tornado. Along the walls waited the demons we had heard, only the instant we set foot inside to the building, their horrible sounds had stopped to leave an oppressive, charged silence broken only by the rattle of Professor Briggs' breath and the tap of his walking stick against the floor.

Dara lay motionless in the middle of the huge room. A circle of green fire surrounded her but didn't touch her, yet. As we watched, it grew tighter, closing on her inch by deadly inch. It was a trap, a taunting, cruel snare set as a twisted joke by Chutka the Shambler.

It was obvious he expected me to climb through the flames to save the girl I loved. His mocking, dancing, bottomless black eyes watched me from the far end of the room. I didn't have to look at him to feel his glee that we had followed him into the realm where he ruled. No mercy would be given to us, and just like the shrinking circle of flames that surrounded Dara, our deaths would be the end result of his game of cat and mouse.

I took a step forward.

"Wait," Briggs said quietly. "I have a plan."

"Thank goodness," Vicken replied. "I was afraid to ask Finn. His plans are the worst."

The professor kept his gaze on the Demon Prince. He spoke quietly so only we could hear. "Vicken, bite Finn. I'll distract Chutka so that you can inject him with Finn's blood like you did to the Darkest Warlock to make him vulnerable. Hopefully, if Finn attacks him, he'll phase into a wolf and they can battle it out while we rescue Dara. Finn's an Alpha. He should be strong enough to keep Chutka at bay until we escape. With any luck, we can hightail it out of here in one piece."

Vicken looked from the professor to me. "Finn, what's your plan?"

As bad as Professor Briggs' idea had been, I really didn't have anything better at the moment. I lifted a shoulder. "To go with the professor's plan."

Vicken shook his head. "That's a horrible plan! I'm disappointed in both of you!"

I threw up my hands. "Then come up with a plan of your own for once instead of criticizing mine all the time! If you think you have something better, let's hear it!"

Vicken looked from me to the professor, then back again. "Fine. We'll go with Briggs' plan, but if we all die, I'm blaming you."

"Fine," I replied. I held out my arm.

Vicken hesitated with his teeth above my skin. "Are you sure about this?" he asked quietly, all pretense of frustration gone in the place of worry.

I nodded. "It's worth a shot. He's weaker with the moonstone. Maybe my blood can give us an edge."

Vicken let out a breath and sunk his teeth into my skin. My teeth ground together at the pain and a tremor ran across my skin, but I kept my face emotionless. The last thing the vampire needed was guilt after everything he had been through. I couldn't believe he was even walking, let alone ready to face Chutka in a very, very pathetic shot of us defeating him.

He lifted his head, gave me one last searching look, and then ducked under Professor Briggs' arm to help him toward Chutka.

"I had to jump through the crack," I heard Vicken mutter under his breath. "Don't follow Finn. Now there's a plan. I really should try that next time. I'll probably live longer."

I agreed with him, but I wouldn't give him the pleasure of hearing it aloud. The last thing Briggs and I needed was to listen to a gloating vampire before we died. And if we didn't die, he would be impossible to live with.

I wondered how Briggs intended on distracting the Demon Prince so Vicken could get close enough to bite him. Though the demons around the room kept silent, they began to sway from side to side as Vicken and Briggs approached their ruler. The demons surged inward, filling the floor between myself and the others, blocking my path. The smell of pain from the professor would excite them. I could only hope Briggs knew what he was doing.

I kept an eye on them as I made my way toward Dara. The flames were getting a little too close to her for my comfort.

"Has anyone ever told you how much you stink?" Briggs asked the Demon Prince.

A low rumble sounded from Chutka. He leaned against the far wall with one massive, clawed hand on his chest where the moonstone had done its damage. I could hear his labored breathing. Maybe we had a chance after all.

But first, I had to figure out how to get Dara out of danger. The fire was almost to her. I could go through it, but my full attention on the flames would leave us both vulnerable to the demons. If Vicken and Briggs got in trouble, I wouldn't be able to help them if I was carrying her. I needed help.

With one eye on my friends, I turned my attention to Sparrow.

"Time to try something, little one," I whispered to her. "Think the other dragons will listen?"

Sparrow licked my chin with her red, forked tongue and flapped her wings to rise into the air. She flew around my head once before using her wings to hover in front of me. I could see how even the short time we had spent apart had changed her. Instead of gawky, spindly legs and wings that appeared too big for her tiny body, she had grown into her limbs and was now a sleek, lithe, graceful creature who appeared at home in the air and in command of her abilities. It made me realize that Professor Seedly had been right about dragons aging quickly; I missed my baby sylph dragon, but was grateful for the poise and readiness that showed in every line of my little friend's posture.

"Fly away with Dara," I whispered and pushed to the dragons. "Get her out of here. Keep her safe."

Sparrow flew near me even as the other dragons soared toward the circle of flames.

I could read the concern in the dragon's gaze, but shook my head. "I'll be okay. I need to know you and Dara are safe. Get her as far from the demons as you can. Protect her. Can you do that?"

Sparrow gave a little puff of mint-scented flame that vanished before it reached me. She circled my head one more time, then flew off to join the others.

They hovered above Dara and the green fire uncertainly. I tried to push away the fact that we stood in a windowless, fire-ceilinged, crumbling-walled room filled with demons and Chutka the Shambler. I heard Professor Brigg's cane tap against the floor as he neared the Demon Prince; at the same time, Brigg's forcingly jovial words said that he was still toying with the Demon Prince. I doubted it would be long before Chutka tired of the professor's chatter.

I closed my eyes and pushed at the dragons again. "Fly away with Dara. Get her out of here. Keep her safe. Follow Sparrow."

"Get away from her," Chutka growled.

I opened my eyes to see the dragons dart down past the circle of flames. Their tiny claws latched onto Dara's shirt and pants. Sparrow gave a little huff of command and the dragons rose into the air. Dara's still form lifted with them.

"Stop them!" Chutka shouted. "Kill her!"

"Don't you dare hurt my students," Professor Briggs said.

He threw his walking stick at the Demon Prince. Chutka batted it away. His attention was distracted only for a split second, but it was long enough. Vicken darted forward with his vampire speed and sunk his teeth into the Demon Prince's huge shoulder. Chutka let out a roar of rage and slapped the vampire away.

Vicken flew into one of the walls. He hit it so hard massive bricks toppled from the top of the wall. When the vampire fell to the ground, the bricks piled on top of him.

"Vicken!" I shouted.

Chutka lunged toward the vampire. It was then that I saw the reason he had been hanging at the back of the long room. His chest had originally been pale and smooth except for the scar where he had taken pieces of his own heart in an attempt to open the gate; but now that smoothness had been eaten away by pockets of sunken, pitted holes. The holes originated over his heart.

Their pattern was familiar. I realized with a start that it was because the pockets and raised ridges were an exact replica of the moon. Somehow, the sphere that revealed the truth of the mythics had also marked itself on the Demon Prince's body. It was as though even the moon wanted to remind Chutka that he didn't belong in our realm.

"Stop the dragons!" Chutka commanded.

The demons leaped into action, but it was too late. The little sylph dragons flapped their wings and lifted Dara well past the reach of the baying, yowling creatures. I could only hope as they carried her through the hole in the doorway that we weren't too late.

Green fire spilled from between the Demon Prince's needle-like teeth and onto the floor. It snaked through the bricks towards Vicken. Vampires had no immunity to the fire. Vicken would burn to death where he lay.

The professor stood in Chutka's path. Hunched over with one hand clutching his bleeding chest and the other a scarred mess from battling the Demon Prince's subordinate, the warlock looked small and pathetic compared to the towering, massive, hooved prince. Yet when Briggs straightened, the haughtiness in his eyes and the anger on his face made him appear ten times bigger than Chutka.

"Don't you dare hurt him!" Professor Briggs growled.

"You can't stop me," Chutka replied.

"That's where you're wrong," Briggs said.

The professor began to chant. Though I didn't know the words, I recognized them immediately. But instead of setting a shield around Vicken, Briggs enveloped himself and the Demon Prince. The green flames that surrounded Chutka surged past the professor's feet, but they couldn't break the barrier of the shield. Trapped, the green flames doubled and raced up the professor's dark robes. His face twisted in pain, but he continued to chant.

"No!" I shouted.

"You'll destroy yourself to save him," Chutka said with a derisive laugh. "But the shield won't hold when your bones are burning. I'll kill them all!"

"Leave him alone!" I shouted.

Demons barred my path. Their gleaming teeth and reaching claws would shred me to pieces if their flames didn't overwhelm me first. As it was, I had to concentrate to remind myself that the flames at my feet had no power over me. If I gave in to the fear, I would lose the battle.

My head jerked up. That was the key. That was how I could stop him.

"Chutka, you already lost."

The Demon Prince threw me a scornful look. "Your beloved professor is dying. You're the one who lost."

I shook my head. "Your heart is damaged; the Demon Knight, the Darkest Warlock, and the Wiccan Enforcer are gone. That must have hurt your pride a bit, not to mention the fact that your hold on my world is slipping." I lifted a shoulder in a half-shrug. "This is the end of everything you started, Chutka. You've failed."

His eyes narrowed. "You're wrong."

But I heard it in his words, the tiny slip, the smallest hint of a weakness. It was fear, and fear was something I could control.

I held up my hands and pushed at Chutka. I might have had no shot before, but my blood flowed through the Demon Prince. A part of him, albeit a small one, was werewolf, and I was the Alpha.

"You lost," I said. I pushed the thought at him with all my might. One side of me heard Professor Briggs cry out in pain he could no longer stifle. The fire was taking over. I didn't have much time. "You set out to take over my world and you failed. You will never, ever succeed."

I glanced down at the demons surrounding me. Channeling my Alpha strength, I lowered a hand to the demons. "Don't touch me," I commanded.

The demons backed away, their expressions confused as they looked from their prince back to me, but they lowered their claws. I stepped through the fire. It took all of my strength to keep the pain at bay while pushing at Chutka. If I lost concentration on either front, my feet would burn the way my palm had done, and the Demon Prince would destroy Briggs and Vicken without mercy. My hands shook with the effort as I took careful steps through the demon horde.

"You lost, Chutka. You're done."

"You're wrong," the Demon Prince protested. But his voice was weak. His clawed hands opened and closed in uncertainty. Though the fire roared around him, he no longer seemed in control of it.

Keeping up the intensity of the push was taking its toll on me and not working fast enough. I switched tactics. I grabbed the memory I wanted and shoved it at Chutka. The memory became our shared reality. I tailored it carefully to avoid giving the Demon Prince any other loved ones he could torment. The darkness swept over me with the memory.

There was a split second between laughter and the sound of the car striking the cement bridge barrier. The car pivoted upward and over the railing. The force of the airbags deploying along with the crash of the car into the water struck so hard I blacked out. I came to at the sensation of icy water flowing past my knees. It took all of my strength to push the door open and force my way out.

The water was so cold it stole my breath and made my muscles seize. Ice floes battered against me. I could barely make out the hood of the car against the dark water. I tried to swim for the shore, but my arms stopped responding to my commands in the icy liquid and my paddling was no longer enough to keep me afloat. I tried to hold onto the car, but my frozen fingers couldn't find a purchase. Exhaustion stole through my sluggish mind. I knew in that moment that I was going to drowned.

Hopelessness swarmed through my mind as black dots danced in my vision. My head sank beneath the water.

My shoes touched the bottom of the river. My body gave a jerk of protest at the air I wasn't able to draw in. Panic filled me, but despite my flailing arms, I couldn't force my way up. My eyes closed against my will and my arms hung suspended in the water. The last bubble of air escaped from my mouth. Darkness filled my mind.

My head jerked up at the realization that I was on my knees in the middle of the demon-filled building. Professor Briggs somehow still kept the shield barrier up despite the fire eating at him. Chutka the Shambler towered over the professor trapped in the shield as well, but in the place of the Demon Prince's usual hungry, merciless expression I read loss and hopelessness. Something glimmered in his eyes. My breath caught in my throat at the realization that I was seeing true fear. The memory had worked.

I grasped onto it with all of my might. I pushed as I shouted, “The fire will devour you, Chutka. The pain is real. It’s hungry. It wants you. It will destroy you.”

Chutka blinked, then turned his head to look at me. The green flames in the depths of the Demon Prince’s gaze flickered and then wavered between the flames and the gold of a werewolf’s reflective irises. When his eyes met mine, they widened. His nostrils flared, and the fire around him turned from Briggs and raced up his hooves and massive legs to the darkness that shrouded him.

The Demon Prince let out a howl of such pain the demons that filled the room yelped and cowered away from him. When another yell tore from Chutka, the demons scurried from the room in droves. Their fires faded away and left me kneeling in the darkness lit only by the Demon Prince’s flame.

“No!” Chutka yelled.

Finding mortal weakness in the Demon Prince’s flesh, the flames devoured everything in their path. Chutka ducked and twisted, but he couldn’t evade the fire that came from himself. The green flames multiplied with the fuel of his fear until they were so bright I had to shield my gaze with my hand. His shouts rose into shrieks and then stopped entirely. He became a roaring pillar that battered me with its heat. A single pinnacle of white light glowed where the moonstone had taken up residence in his heart. The green and white light warred until every inch of the room was lit up. Then, with a hissing pop, the light vanished completely.

I rose shakily to my feet, but I couldn’t see anything even with my werewolf eyesight. Silence filled the air, but it was thick and muffled as though the entire building had been filled with cotton. A sulfurous, burned-flesh smell hung heavy in the room. I had no sense of direction and no way of knowing if I was about to be attacked by Chutka's demons. A moan sounded in the darkness. I couldn't tell in the strange silence if it came from Vicken, Professor Briggs, or Chutka the Shambler. With tense muscles and gritted teeth, I made my way toward it.

My fingers brushed rubble. I fell to my knees and scrambled at the massive bricks. Something stirred beneath them.

"Hang on," I said, hoping Vicken could hear me. "I'll get you out."

I reached for a brick and pulled. Something grabbed my hand. I jerked back in surprise.

"Finn?" came Vicken's weak voice.

I grabbed his hand. "It's me. Hold on."

I shoved my shoulder against the top brick. It fell with a muted thud to the side. Straining, I shoved two more away. Reaching down, I searched for Vicken in the darkness. My hand brushed the cloth of his shirt. One hand grabbed mine, then another.

"I'm going to pull," I told him.

"Do it," he replied, his voice tight.

I channeled the weak remains of my werewolf strength that had been sapped in my mental assault against Chutka and pulled backwards. Vicken struggled with me. Small gasps of pain sounded from the vampire, but he didn't let go. The hairs on the back of my neck prickled and I felt as though at any moment a horde of angry demons was about to attack me. I kept working until, inch by inch, we freed Vicken from the rubble.

"Help me stand," my friend said.

I could smell blood. I didn't know if it was coming from him or if it was from him biting me. I ducked under his arm and eased him carefully to his feet. A slight intake of breath was the only the sign he gave of his pain. I felt him waver when

I stepped back. Without a word, I pulled his arm over my shoulder again. We stood side by side staring into the impenetrable darkness.

"Where's Briggs?" Vicken asked. "Is Chutka still out there?"

"I don't know," I said in answer to both questions. "I think—"

I stopped speaking at the sight of a light in the darkness. It was faint and blue, barely bright enough to penetrate the depths.

"What is that?" Vicken whispered.

"I'm not sure," I replied. "I'll go check it out."

I stepped away from him with the intention of leaving him there in case the light signified more danger, but Vicken grabbed my shoulder.

"I'm coming with you."

Step by careful step, we cleared the rubble of the bricks and made our way toward the faint blue light. When we drew closer, I watched the blue separate into three lines. After a few more steps, my werewolf eyesight made out scrolled letters.

Trace Nathaniel Briggs.

"No," I said before I realized I had even spoken.

"What is it?" Vicken asked.

One more step was all it took to change my fears into reality.

Alden knelt next to a motionless form. His head was bowed and tears showed on his cheeks. The name that glowed on his arm lit up Professor Briggs' pale face. His eyes were closed and his eyebrows were pulled together as though he was in intense pain. The scar down his cheek appeared harsh in the faint light.

I lowered slowly to the ground on Briggs' other side. Vicken used my shoulder to help ease himself down next to me.

Briggs' labored breathing came harshly to my ears. I couldn't see his legs or arms in the darkness, but I knew by the charred smell that the demon fire had taken a lethal toll.

"Is he…," Vicken began.

Alden shook his head. "Not yet," the Grim said quietly. He wiped his eyes and looked at me. "But your uncle…."

Pain overwhelmed my heart. I couldn't stop the tears that overflowed my eyes and rolled down my cheeks. "Did he…did he suffer?" I asked past the knot that had tightened in my throat.

"Not in the end," Alden replied. "I stopped it." He sniffed, then said, "Your mother was waiting for him. She said she was proud of him. He couldn't stop smiling."

I nodded and lowered my gaze to the professor. Hundreds of moments we had shared together in my short time at Haunted High flooded my mind. His hatred, his indifference, his kindness, and eventually, his friendship had shaped my ability to cope with being a werewolf. The thought of losing him was nearly unbearable. Yet, after all he had gone through, he deserved to be free.

Professor Briggs' eyes opened. He looked past us to a place in the darkness.

"Zanie?"

His voice was a croak of both pain and wonder. A smile touched his lips. The tears that trailed down his scarred cheek fell to the ground with little, muffled patters.

"She's here," Alden said, following the professor's gaze.

I looked into the darkness with the hope of seeing the ghost who had helped us, but there was nothing. I lifted a trembling hand to my face and wiped my tears.

"P-please take care of him, Mezania," I said in a voice that refused to be steady.

Vicken's hand tightened on my shoulder and I heard the vampire choke back a sob. "Yes," he said. "Take care of him."

Professor Briggs' gaze sharpened and for a brief moment, his eyes shifted from the darkness to us.

"My boys," he said, his voice barely a whisper.

He held out a burned hand. Vicken and I both took it.

"We're here," I told him.

He gave us a warm smile. "You did good."

I sniffed. "But we couldn't save you."

A single tear followed the others down his cheek. "I made my choice."

I took a shuddering breath. "But what will we do without you?"

The professor's brow furrowed. "Create more trouble, I suppose." He chuckled and then winced at the pain. His eyes closed.

I tightened my grip on his hand and closed my eyes against more tears. I wished I could share his pain the way Dara was able to. I couldn't bear the thought of going back to the Academy without the professor. It would feel empty and strange without his presence.

"Finn?"

I opened my eyes and met the professor's gaze once more. He gave me a knowing smile. "You don't stink." His eyes shifted to Vicken. "Neither of you do. You're good boys. Live…." His voice caught and he winced before he concluded, "Live good lives."

"We will," Vicken said, his voice broken.

"We will," I echoed.

Professor Briggs' gaze clouded. He looked past me to the darkness again. "I'm coming, Zanie," he whispered. "I'm finally coming home."

He sighed. The breath that rattled in his throat left to never return. The professor's head lolled gently on the floor. Alden put a hand on his forehead and closed his eyes. As we watched, the pair brightened with a brilliant blue glow, and then Alden disappeared, leaving us in darkness once more.

It took Vicken and I several minutes to collect ourselves. We leaned against each other there on the stone floor with the professor's broken body until scratching sounds in the darkness brought us to the present.

"We need to go," Vicken said.

"How do we know which way?" I asked.

As if in answer, another light appeared. This one was purple-hued and further away, but it moved back and forth as if searching for something.

A slight, pained smile touched my mouth when I recognized what it was.

"Sparrow," I called thickly.

Chapter Fourteen

THE LIGHT TURNED AND sped straight toward us. As soon as Sparrow reached me, she darted around me from top to bottom as though searching for injury. On finding only minor wounds, the dragon landed on my shoulder and pushed her head gently against my face.

"I'm glad to see you, too," I forced out past my tight throat. "Do you know where the gate is?"

The dragon leaped from my shoulder and flew in front of me. I knelt to gather the professor's body in my arms. With Vicken leaning against my shoulder for support, I made my way carefully after Sparrow. She flew on ahead and then retreated back to us, covering the distance at least a dozen times before we were ready to move on. Our progress was slow in the darkness, but with the dragon's light, at least it was a bit easier. The scratching sound in the distance stayed at bay, but my instincts warned that if we didn't get out of there soon, we would be prey to whatever watched us from the deep shadows.

More lights heralded the dragons waiting near Dara's unconscious form. They had carried her to a haze and waited around her body in a protective circle. As we drew closer, the haze behind them solidified to form an iridescent wall. A jagged line down the middle showed where the crack had been, but it was sealed tight. Brack's warning that they wouldn't be able to open it again surfaced in my mind.

I laid the professor's body carefully on the floor and then knelt by Dara. The dragons parted to let me close to her. Their small forms crowded anxiously around me.

"Thank you," I told them.

I touched Dara's cheek gently. She didn't respond.

"Is she alright?" Vicken asked.

I glanced back at where the vampire leaned against the haze wall. With the light of the other dragons, I could see the blood that streaked the side of his face and the dull sheen to his eyes. He looked as though he was barely standing.

"I don't know," I replied. "She's unconscious. I don't know what Chutka did to her."

"Maybe bringing her to this place was enough," Vicken said with a meaningful look around. "It feels…wrong. Maybe as an empath, she can't handle it."

I nodded. The same creepy-crawling feeling had been pressing against me. I felt as though I wanted to run away or curl into a ball and stay there forever to hide from this strange, dark place. We didn't belong, that much was certain.

"The sooner we get out of here, the better," I replied. "But how?"

I studied the crack. There was no sign of a break. I ran my fingers down it to the bottom, and then paused.

"What's this?"

Vicken leaned closer. "Are those claw marks?"

I traced a set of four claws away from the crack. A tiny bit of light showed through.

"Yes, demon claws. But where are the demons?" I asked.

Sparrow gave a tiny huff from her seat on my shoulder. Her small blue flame puffed away from her into the darkness. Before it dissipated, it revealed a single form on the floor. The lump didn't move. I took a step closer.

"Is that a demon?" Vicken asked.

Sparrow huffed again. This time, the other dragons blew tiny flames as well. A multitude of colors spouted out from our circle to light the area beyond.

"Demons," I said. "Hundreds of them."

"Thousands," Vicken corrected.

The flames did indeed reveal demons, but they were motionless and lying in huge, unmoving piles. It appeared as though they had fought to reach the crack before Chutka died. His final breath had become theirs as well. It was everything I had hoped for, except—

"They almost made it," Vicken said. "They could have."

The realization that the demons could have made it back through the crack before they died was a terrifying one. If the flame had taken one moment longer to devour Chutka, or if our team had been unable to keep the crack shut past their struggles, we would have failed and they would have swarmed the world.

"But without the demons, we're stuck here," Vicken said. He met my gaze with defeat on his face. "We killed Chutka, and by doing so, we killed ourselves."

He slid to a seated position against the haze. The weary acceptance of his expression ate at me.

"Vicken," I began.

He shook his head. "No. Don't you see? This is how it was supposed to end." He opened a pale hand to indicate the demons. "We started out to defeat them, and we did it."

"But we're supposed to survive," I replied.

He let out a flat, humorless laugh, and then winced. After a moment of silence, he said, "Good vanquishes evil. The hero destroys the bad guy." He looked up at me. "You ran headlong into this one, and came out on top." The light faded from his gaze when he said, "It's not your fault that on top also meant being locked away in some dark, demon reality until we're killed by whatever else is out there."

His words sent a shiver down my spine. "You heard them, too?"

He nodded. "It doesn't take a werewolf's ears to know that there's a whole lot more evil here than just Chutka." A slight smile touched his lips. "At least Brack is good at keeping things closed."

I looked from Dara's unconscious form back to the vampire. The thought that my friends would die because of me made my heart ache. I walked around the circle of light from the dragons until doing so made me dizzy, then I walked in the other direction. I searched for anything that would get us out of there. The problem was that I didn't know any spells or chants, and I didn't have the skills of a warlock to use them even if I knew them. There wasn't any form of weapon I could wield against the wall. Even the dragons wearied of my pacing and eventually settled in around Vicken. The vampire went so far as to run a finger down the back of an orange and green one.

"I'm sorry, guys," he told them. "You were brave. You don't deserve to die down here."

The thought of Sparrow being taken by whatever waited in the darkness made me mad. I grabbed one of the demon's bodies and carried it back to the wall.

"What are you doing?" Vicken asked with mild interest.

I shoved one of the demon's claws against the crack.

"Anything I can," I replied. "I'm not giving up."

The crack didn't show any sign of breaking down beneath my efforts. Whatever power the demon's claws had once had on the gate had apparently vanished with its death. But I tried until I was too weary to hold up the creature any longer. Defeated, I dropped it at my feet and slumped to a seated position beside Vicken. My foot touched the dead demon's body, but I no longer had the strength to care.

"This isn't the way it's supposed to end," I said with my head in my hands. "You aren't supposed to follow me to your death."

Vicken surprised me by patting my shoulder. "I told myself that not following you would probably keep me alive."

I gave him a dry look. "You should have followed that plan."

He shook his head. "And be locked up there never knowing what happened? We defeated Chutka the Shambler and we protected our world from the demons." He smiled. "We did exactly what we set out to do."

"We didn't set out to die," I pointed out.

He lifted a shoulder. "Like I said, you need to work on your plans." His gaze shifted to the dead demon at my feet. "If the demons could have gotten through in time, they would have. We're lucky your werewolf blood is so susceptible to burning."

That brought a wry laugh from me. I sat back against the wall and lifted my hand to view the barely discernable burn on my palm. "Yeah, lucky."

Vicken's answering chuckle faded away to silence. I had just about closed my eyes when he sat up. I looked at him to find his gaze on the demon once more.

"If they could have gotten through, they would have," he repeated.

"You already said that," I pointed out.

He lifted a hand to silence me. "I have a plan."

"Why do I think I'm not going to like it?" I replied warily.

Vicken didn't look at me. "You've done enough stupid things. My turn."

"What are you talking about?" I asked.

Vicken pulled the demon toward him. "Don't try to stop me."

"Stop you from doing what?" I asked, alarmed.

Vicken lowered his head to the demon's throat. "This," he said before he sunk his teeth into the creature's jugular.

"Vicken, stop!" I protested.

I grabbed the demon and tried to pull it away, but the vampire held the body in his vicelike grip as he took several deep gulps of the creature's blood.

When he finally lifted his head, blood streaked his chin. "That's what I thought," he said.

"What?" I asked with concern.

"Demon blood is nasty," he replied. He gave a choking sound and the demon body fell from his hands.

"Vick!" I grabbed his arm.

Vicken pushed me away. He fell to his knees in the middle of the circle of light from the dragons and bent over, gagging.

"Not…pleasant…," he gasped out.

I took a step toward him, but he held out a hand. I stopped at the look on his face.

"Demons can open the gate," he said, his breath coming quickly. "So I become the demon and open it."

I shook my head. "That's madness."

He gave me a wild, crazy look. "So is letting you die here."

I stared at him. "You came here because of me! I'm the reason we're going to die!"

He clenched his teeth. "Not if I can help it."

He doubled over and grabbed his stomach. A cry of pain tore from him. I reached out a hand to touch his shoulder, but he jerked back. A wail escaped him that turned into a yowl so similar to the demons' that fear sent tingles along my arms. I couldn't defeat Vicken at full strength. What if he couldn't control the demon and turned on us?

I backed away to place myself between Vicken, Dara, and the dragons. Sparrow hissed a warning from my shoulder.

At the sound, Vicken straightened with his back to us. Spikes poked through his shirt. His knees lengthened and became jointed strangely, and when he rose to full height, he was taller than he had been. I could see an extra joint at his elbows that popped when he opened them. I sucked in a breath.

Vicken turned. My heart slowed. His eyes were larger than they had been and they were black and filled with green flames. His cheeks were sunken and hollow. His mouth opened and when he panted, I saw rows of pointed needle-like teeth where his fangs had been. He sucked in rapid breaths and wove his head from side to side like a snake. With his hair out of its band and hanging to his shoulders, his black tee-shirt tattered, and limbs double jointed, he looked like something out of my darkest nightmare. I had to tell myself that he was my friend. I wouldn't fear him.

"V-Vicken?" I said.

He took a step toward me. Claws had forced their way through the toes of his favorite black leather shoes. The sound of them scratching on the ground with the step made my muscles tighten. I lifted my hands in an unconscious effort to keep him from Dara.

Vicken stopped. He looked from me to Dara's still form without blinking. It unsettled me to see the predatory cast to his gaze. Never in my time in the demon realm had I thought that maybe the creature to fear in the darkness was the friend I had come to trust.

That thought solidified when Vicken took a step forward and then another. I backed up to stand in front of Dara. The dragons hid behind me. I could hear their little breaths of fear.

They had been so brave. They didn't deserve to die in this evil realm.

"He won't hurt us," I told them. "Trust him. It's going to be alright."

Vicken didn't appear to hear me. The dragons backed away at his approach. They covered Dara with their wings and puffed little clouds of flame, but Vicken ignored them as well. He advanced with slow, scratching steps.

"Vicken, stop," I commanded when he was less than two feet from us.

He could have reached out a clawed hand and torn my heart from my chest. I wasn't sure if I would have fought him.

Vicken merely looked at me, his gaze demonic and at the same time so familiar I told myself over and over that he wouldn't hurt anyone.

Vicken turned away with slow movements as though he was fighting inside of himself. I let out the breath I hadn't known I'd been holding. Vicken lifted a clawed hand to the crack in the wall. He put a single claw to it and brought it down slowly like a child scraping frost from a window. The mist peeled away to let in a tiny sliver of light. Vicken lifted his hand again and scratched downward. More lights appeared. Relief flooded me. I knelt next to Dara and the dragons.

"Vicken's got this," I told them.

Vicken put both clawed hands to the wall. A grunt escaped him as he shoved his claws into the haze. With a rumble from deep within his chest, he drew his claws downward to cause a long gash.

Light spilled through the gloomy darkness. Vicken hissed and stepped back as though it hurt his skin. I realized it must have been moonlight from his reaction.

"You've got this," I told him. "You're almost there."

Vicken turned his head to look at me. The familiarity of his gaze had been almost completely overtaken by the demon.

Confusion warred with determination on his face. I was losing him.

"Keep clawing the wall," I told him. I rose to my feet. "Break through. You can do this. You can make it."

Vicken looked back at the claw marks. He looked from them to his hands.

"That's it," I urged. "You've got this, Vicken. Don't give up!"

As if his name jarred his mind back into focus, Vicken clawed at the wall with a strength that terrified and amazed me. The crack grew deeper and more pronounced. I glimpsed the main corridor beyond where students and professors from the Academy waited.

But then it vanished. The crack began to close despite Vicken's efforts.

I remembered Vicken's mention of Brack's affinity.

"Brack!" I yelled. "Brack, it's us! You've got to let us through!"

The crack lessened even more. Vicken clawed at it, but he couldn't get it to widen.

Desperate to get out, I changed my tactic and focused my thoughts on the werewolves. Pushing with all of my might, I said, "Stop Brack. We need to get through. He's trapping us here!"

The crack lessened for the space of another heartbeat, and then paused.

"That's it," I breathed.

Vicken shoved his claws in the crack and pulled. It widened, but barely. He shoved his claws deeper and tried to force it apart. A snarl escaped him as he put his entire strength behind it, but the crack's movement was almost imperceptible.

I reached Vicken's side. He looked down at me. I held his gaze, searching for my friend beneath the demon.

"I trust you, Vicken," I said quietly.

I put my hands to the crack and pushed. After a moment, Vicken's claws joined me. Together, we clawed, shoved, struggled, and grunted as we forced the crack wide enough to accommodate a single person. The moment we let go, the crack began to close again with maddening strength.

Vicken strained to hold it open. "Go," he grunted.

I let go and ran to Dara's side. "Come on!" I told the dragons. I gathered Dara up in my arms and ran back to the crack. Ducking in sideways, I forced my way through. A hiss escaped Vicken as the effort to hold the tear open became too great.

Staring students and wide-eyed professors met me on the other side.

"Take her!" I shouted as soon as I reached the corridor.

Hands grabbed Dara and tried to pull me through, too.

"Not yet," I told them.

I shoved my shoulders back inside the crack and reached until my hand closed on Vicken's clawed one. He pulled back.

"I…stay," I heard him say.

A growl escaped me. "There's no way I'm letting you stay there," I replied.

I grabbed his other hand and yanked him forward. The crack closed as I fell backwards. I felt it press against my body, threatening to shut us inside. Hands pulled me from the corridor. Vicken let out a yell of pain as something else grabbed him from the demon realm. With a final yell, I pulled back with all of my might.

Vicken and I fell from the crack and collapsed in a heap on the floor of the Academy.

I looked up to see Brack staring down at us with wide eyes.

"Close it!" I gasped.

The warlock motioned with one hand. The crack above us closed with a resolute snap and then vanished altogether.

"Demon!" someone shouted.

"Start the chant!" another said.

"No!" I yelled.

I pushed to my feet, shielding Vicken with my body. A glance back showed that anything familiar about my friend had vanished to leave a cowering, confused, long-limbed demon behind. My heart fell.

"This is Vicken," I said as much to convince myself as to warn them.

"Finn, are you sure?"

I looked up to see Professor Mellon and the Headmistress looking at the demon. Mercer stood behind them with the closest thing to a worried expression I had ever seen on his face.

I nodded. "I'm sure. We've got to banish the demon from his body. You must know how."

I looked from one of them to the other in desperation.

First Professor Mellon, then the Headmistress, and finally Mercer shook their heads. The other professors that stood in front of the students lowered their gazes.

"There isn't a chant for that," the Headmistress said.

Fear filled me. "There must be something!"

"Finn, look out!"

I glanced back as the demon lunged with his mouth open. Rhett and another werewolf named Cameron tackled him before he could reach me. The other werewolves joined them, pinning the demon down.

"Don't hurt him," I said.

"What do we do with him?" Rhett asked, his voice tight as he struggled to keep from being sliced open by one of Vicken's claws.

I looked around quickly. My gaze landed on the shredded unicorn photograph the demons had destroyed. "The basement. Hurry. Brack, show them where it is."

They half-dragged, half-carried the spitting, clawing, protesting demon toward the hidden door the warlock opened. The sound of their struggle down the stairs faded to leave a room scented in fear and panic. I turned my gaze back to the professors.

"There must be a way. He sacrificed himself for us!" I pleaded.

Mercer nodded. "We'll start searching. Where's Briggs?"

The thought of the professor made my knees go weak. "He, uh...." I glanced at the crack. The fact that I had left his body behind in the demon realm made my shoulders start to shake. "He helped kill Chutka. But the fire...the fire...." I couldn't force the words out.

A hand touched my shoulder. For a moment, for just a happy, split-reality moment, I thought it was Professor Briggs comforting me.

I turned to see Mercer with understanding in his usually impassive eyes. "It's alright, Finn."

I shook my head. "It's not alright. He died to protect us, and now he's there and he's, he's...."

"He's not there."

I looked over at the sound of Alden's voice.

The Grim met my gaze through the mass of students. They parted to let him through. "He's home, Finn. He's where he wants to be."

I looked from my friend to where Professor Rexus held Dara in his huge arms. His horns dwarfed the girl.

I forced myself to ask Alden the question I was dreading. It was hard to keep the accusation out of my voice. "And what about Dara? Do you have her name, too?"

Alden pulled up his sleeve to show me his bare arm. Relief filled me with such sharpness that I could barely breathe. I must have looked as close to falling over as I felt because the Headmistress ducked under my arm.

"Come on, Finn," she said. "Let's get both of you upstairs. We'll deal with Vicken after we've had a chance to check on you."

I allowed myself to be led upstairs. The sounds of the professors reassuring the students were followed by footsteps. I couldn't help the feeling that we were leaving someone behind. I closed my eyes to keep back the tears.

Chapter Fifteen

MOVEMENT MADE MY EYES open. I lifted my head from where I had leaned my face in my hand and apparently fallen asleep. Eyes met mine. Their violet hue deepened when she smiled. The stark white of the pillowcase was counterbalanced by Dara's long ashen hair and the hospital gown Dr. Six had dressed her in. The sight of her awake made me want to smile and cry at the same time.

"Hello, beautiful," I said.

"I love you," she replied.

I stared at her. When I had first professed my love, she had told me she refused to give her heart to anyone. She had been hurt too deeply by those she loved, and she refused to put herself in that situation again.

I shook my head, scarcely daring to believe my ears. "You love me?"

Dara's smile faded slightly. "When Chutka took me, I thought I was going to die. My only regret, the only one, was that I had been afraid to tell you how I felt." She lifted a soft hand to my cheek. "I'm not afraid anymore."

I covered her hand with my own and told her, "I love you with all of my heart, Dara."

She tipped her head when she looked at me. "You're sad."

I forced a smile. "I'm happy you're alright. I've been so afraid I would lose you. I haven't left your side."

"We won?" she asked.

I nodded.

"But it was hard," she said, guessing what I didn't want to say.

I lowered my gaze. "Really hard. Professor Briggs was killed, Uncle Conrad died, and Vicken's a demon. He sacrificed himself to get us out of the demon realm. The professors and our team have been working nonstop, but we haven't been able to find a way to free him from the demon form." I swallowed past my tight throat. "His soul is dying."

"His soul?" Dara repeated.

I nodded. "Mercer said that a demon is a creature without a heart or soul, which is why it lives to devour fear and pain. That's all it can feel." I took in a slow breath and said, "Vicken's soul can't survive the demon form. Even now, there's nothing left of him I recognize." I couldn't meet her gaze. "He's dying, Dara."

"Maybe I can help," she replied, rising to a sitting position.

I set a hand on her arm, afraid that she would push herself too far after all she had been through.

"Maybe you should wait."

She shook her head. "Vicken sacrificed for us. If there's anything we can do to save him, we need to do it."

Before I could protest, she rose from the bed. She staggered slightly and looked like she was going to fall. Without giving her the chance to deny my help, I picked her up in my arms.

She smiled up at me. "That was pretty smooth, Mr. Briscoe."

I couldn't help the smile that spread across my face. "I have my moments."

"Yes, you do," she agreed as I made my way to the door.

I carried her down the stairs to the main corridor. It was empty at the late hour; only a faint, charred scent remained to tell of the terror we had survived the night before. I stepped through the tattered remains of the unicorn photograph the demons had destroyed and walked slowly down the steps with Dara in my arms. The fact that she let me carry her told of the weakness she kept hidden. Dr. Six had confirmed Vicken's worry that the demon realm had taken its toll on the empath. I hoped being near the vampire wasn't going to affect her in a bad way.

I had spent the last day between the door to the basement room and waiting at Dara's side for her to awaken. The sound of Vicken's labored breathing beyond told me that he was still in the demon form. When we approached the door, his claws raked the inside with a sound like fingernails on a chalkboard. It set my teeth on edge.

"Vicken?" Dara called out.

The scratching intensified. She shot me a worried look as I lowered her onto the steps. I sat beside her.

"Brack used his affinity on the door. Vicken can't get out. The last time we opened it to check on him, he nearly removed one of Professor Rexus' horns. Luckily, Dr. Six was able to fix it. He's up in the infirmary sleeping off the effects of her crystals. I promised the Headmistress I wouldn't let anyone open the door again until we found a cure for Vicken."

The Headmistress had used the word *unless*, not *until*, but I didn't tell Dara that. I was determined to do everything I could to help Vicken if it was the last thing I did.

Footsteps sounded on the stairs above us and Dara stiffened.

"It's alright," I told her.

Kiyah appeared. She paused when she saw us, then continued down.

"Back here, huh?" she asked with forced lightness when she lowered to the step above mine.

"I guess I keep hoping being close to him will give me ideas. What about you?" I asked.

Kiyah nodded. Her silver and pink streaked hair brushed her shoulders. "The same. The entire pack is searching. I think Rhett's read more books today than he ever has in his life."

That brought a small smile from me. "That'll be good for him." I followed her questioning gaze to Dara. "I forget you two haven't met. Dara, this is Kiyah. She's one of the werewolves from the Den. She helped save Vicken's life." I smiled at Kiyah and said before I could stop myself, "Dara's my girlfriend and she just told me she loved me."

Dara laughed and pushed my shoulder. I gave her a lopsided grin.

Kiyah smiled. "Pleased to meet you. Any friend of Finn's is someone I've found worth knowing, especially if you love him."

Dara threw me a smile. "I do."

Kiyah nodded. "He deserves it. He's a good guy."

I caught Dara's questioning look and chuckled. "Don't worry. Kiyah's feelings aren't for me." I gestured toward the door. "They're for him."

Dara's eyes widened. "You love Vicken?"

Kiyah nodded as her smile faded. “I do. With all of my heart.” She glanced at me. “It’s a werewolf thing. I know loving a vampire doesn’t make any sense, but—”

“But the heart wants what it wants,” Dara concluded as she slipped her hand into mine.

Kiyah nodded. “Exactly.” She turned her gaze on the door. “But the vampire I love isn’t in there.”

“He’s there,” Dara reassured her. “I can still feel him.”

Relief made the tension ease in my shoulders. “You can?”

Dara nodded. “I can, but it’s faint. He’s not going to be there long.” The worry showed in her violet gaze when she looked up at me. “What are we going to do?”

“I don’t know,” I admitted. “We’re running out of time and we have no options. Everything the professors have tried has failed. I don’t know what else to do.”

I shied away from the thought of losing Vicken completely to the demons. We had sacrificed so much to defeat Chutka. It didn’t feel fair that Vicken’s life would be sacrificed as well.

Something touched my shoulder. I looked up expecting to see Kiyah’s hand, but she was leaning against the opposite wall with her gaze on the door.

Dara caught my questioning look. “What?”

“Did you touch my shoulder?” I asked, even though doing so meant she would have had to lean across the stairway awkwardly to do it.

She shook her head. “No. Why?”

I frowned. “I felt someone there. It doesn’t make sense.” Something poked my shoulder in the same place. I jumped up. “There it is again.”

I stared at the empty staircase.

“What’s going on?” Kiyah asked.

“Something’s messing with Finn,” Dara replied with confusion in her voice. “But nothing’s there.”

"After everything you've been through, I'm not surprised you're seeing things," Kiyah said.

I shook my head. "I'm not seeing things, I'm feeling them. It's like somebody's trying to get my attention. But there's nobody there, just…." A thought occurred to me. "Cadish."

"Who's Cadish?" Dara asked.

I stared up the staircase. "My mother's imaginary friend that she brought to life. Nobody else can see him, but I think he's been helping me since I got here."

Dara set a hand on my arm. "Finn, you're not making any sense."

Out of the corner of my eye, I saw the empath and werewolf exchange worried glances, but I kept my gaze on the stairs.

"It makes perfect sense," I replied. "My mother helped bring Cadish to life, but something went wrong. One of the moonstones broke and he vanished, but she said he was still there." I sucked in a breath. "Uncle Conrad told me Cadish was just happy my mother had helped him gain a soul." My eyes widened and I repeated, "They helped him gain a soul!"

"What are you talking about?" Kiyah asked.

But Dara had risen at my words. She stared with me up the empty staircase. "How did they do it?"

"With moonstones," I replied. "Lots of moonstones."

"We're supposed to get that shipment from Madam Opal. Do you think it's arrived yet?" Dara asked.

I looked at her and saw the same excitement I felt reflected in her eyes. "I'm not sure, but I'm going to find out!"

I left the girls and ran up the stair four at a time. I burst into Mrs. Hassleton's office and skidded to a stop at the sight of her sorting through files on her desk.

"Finnley Briscoe, what are you doing in here?" she demanded.

"What are you doing in here?" I asked. "It's really late."

"Really early," she corrected. "The Headmistress is a night owl, remember? I keep her hours."

"Right," I replied. "I'm sorry to barge in, but has a box arrived from Madam Opal?"

"You're asking about mail at this time of the morning?" she said, her tone suspicious. "What's gotten into you?"

"I don't have time to explain, but a student's life hangs in the balance. Did you get the package?"

"Well, yes, actually." Mrs. Hassleton looked around her office. "It's here somewhere, I'm sure."

I sniffed as I looked, searching for the smell of ironwood. Mrs. Hassleton batted me away.

"You and your werewolf kind shouldn't be in here, Mr. Briscoe. There are plenty of other schools where—"

"Schools?" I replied, caught off-guard. "You think we should leave the Academy? All of us?"

Mrs. Hassleton paused in the act of shuffling through a stack of oddly shaped packages in the corner. She glanced back at me. "Did I say schools? I meant rooms. Your kind has plenty of rooms here at the Academy. You don't have to be in my office."

I approached her desk. "Mrs. Hassleton, what do you have against werewolves?"

She picked up a spray bottle and aimed it at me. The word 'cloves' was written down the side. "Nothing. You are a student and should be off learning, not harassing me."

I put my hands on her desk. "Mrs. Hassleton, I'm trying to save my best friend's life. In fact, I haven't done anything except try to save this school since I've been here. I've been stabbed, burned, beaten, had my arm broken, and nearly died more times than I could count, and all because I care about this place." I narrowed my eyes at her. "So what makes me being here so wrong?"

Mrs. Hassleton was quiet for a few minutes. The spray bottle lowered along with her gaze. When she spoke, there was a slight hesitation in her voice. "I'm afraid of dogs."

I fought back the urge to laugh hysterically. Finding the moonstones to save Vicken's life was so urgent. The fact that I was now faced with such a paltry fear made me feel as if I was on the edge of going crazy. "Dogs?"

Mrs. Hassleton nodded without looking at me. "I was attacked by a little poodle when I was a toddler." She lifted a hand to her cheek and touched a small triangle-shaped scar I hadn't noticed there. "I had to get stitches and spent a week in the hospital. I've been terrified of them ever since." She lifted her gaze to look at me. "When I see you, all I see is a huge dog waiting to attack."

The realness of her fears smothered any urge I had to laugh. I nodded and shoved my hands in my pockets in an effort to appear less frightening.

"Can I tell you something?" I asked her.

Mrs. Hassleton nodded. The embarrassment she felt at her admission showed in her eyes. It made what I was going to say that much easier.

"When I phased into a werewolf for the first time, I was afraid of myself," I admitted.

Mrs. Hassleton's eyes widened behind her thick glasses. "You-you were?"

I nodded. "Terrified, actually. I didn't even know monsters existed, and then I was suddenly in the form of this nightmarish creature everyone was afraid of, and I couldn't blame them."

"You couldn't?" she said.

"I couldn't," I replied. "I was scared, I was alone, and I had nowhere to turn until I found this place." I lifted a hand from my pocket to indicate the Academy. "Haunted High has become my sanctuary, and I've worked hard to help keep it safe for all of the students here." I met her gaze. "But I don't want someone to be afraid of staying here because of me. Maybe we could find a way to be friends?"

Mrs. Hassleton appeared taken aback. She stared at me with her mouth open and one of her hands raised halfway to her glasses as though she had been about to adjust them and forgot.

"I promise I will never scare you as a wolf and I will make sure none of the other werewolves do, either." I winked at her. "They have to listen to me, you know."

A slight, timid smile touched the woman's mouth. "Do they, really?"

I nodded. "They do, and I'll make sure none of them scare you, ever. I'll tell them they'll be expelled from Haunted High if they do. Will that help you feel better?"

Mrs. Hassleton gave a short nod, paused, and then nodded again. "Yes, actually. That will. That helps a great deal." A relieved expression filled her face. "A great, great deal."

I smiled at her. "And I promise to keep up my end of our friendship. I've been fighting to protect everyone at Haunted High, and that includes you."

That made her smile deepen. "Thank you, Mr. Briscoe."

"I'm glad I can help." I lifted my gaze to the packages behind her. "Now what I need is the package from Madam Opal of the Maes so I can help my friend Vicken. He's going to die if we don't do something."

Mrs. Hassleton's eyes widened. "Vicken Ruvine, the vampire?"

I nodded.

She turned quickly to the packages. "Vicken is such a nice boy. You do everything you can to help him." She picked up a box. "This is the one you're looking for."

I couldn't help staring when she handed it to me. I had never expected the woman who feared me so much to refer to Vicken as such a nice boy.

"Now you take care of him," Mrs. Hassleton directed, shooing me out the door. "If you need anything else to save him, you come right back here, you hear?" She shut the door behind me and left me staring at it.

"Right back here!" Mrs. Hassleton repeated through the door.

I walked numbly to the unicorn photograph and was about to duck inside when Alden called my name.

"Hey, Finn! What are you doing?"

The Grim's voice jolted me back to the present. "Alden, is Vicken's name on your arm yet?"

Alden pushed his sleeve up. For the briefest second, I saw Vicken's name written there in scrolling blue words. I blinked and it was gone. The memory of the same image from the Mythic Labs made my heart pound harder.

"Nope," Alden said with relief in his voice that hinted of how hard it had been to take Professor Briggs away.

"Good," I told him. "Get the others. We have a chant to perform."

"What chant?" Alden asked in surprise.

I held up the box. "A moonstone chant. We're going to save Vicken."

"Where did you find the chant?" the little Grim asked with relief on his face.

"It's my mother's," I replied. "I'll explain when everyone's together."

It didn't take long for the team to meet on the basement steps. They were each as anxious to get Vicken back as I was. Everyone waited eagerly as the sounds of Vicken's scratching increased.

"What's the plan?" Lyris asked.

I held up the box. "These are moonstones from Madam Opal. We're going to use them to bring Vicken's soul back so he can defeat the demon."

"He's going to fight the demon himself?" Lorne asked.

Dara nodded. "If we can help him be strong enough, that's Finn's plan."

"So where do we start?" Kiyah asked.

Everyone looked at me. For the first time, the enormity of what I wanted to accomplish was daunting. I cleared my throat nervously. "We're going to ask if my mother's imaginary friend that she brought to life and gave a soul will help us."

Glances were exchanged. Fortunately, Kiyah and Dara had my back.

"Clear your minds," Kiyah instructed. "Give him a chance to speak."

Dara nodded. "It's difficult for those without a solid form to make themselves heard. We need to be open. Let go of your judgments and your fears, and hold onto your hope for Vicken. Do this for him."

To my relief, every member of the team closed their eyes. I listened to their breathing and their heartbeats settle. The sound of Vicken's harsh breaths in the room beyond came as a stark counterbalance to the stillness of the group. I hoped there was a chance Cadish would speak to us, but I didn't know where to begin.

Dara's hand slipped into mine. She must have sensed my uncertainty, because she spoke in a calm, quiet voice. "Cadish, we need your help. Our friend is fighting for his life, and you have the only key to saving him. Please let us know if you hear us."

I strained every sense toward hearing the spirit or ghost or entity, or whatever Cadish was. The fact that I had no idea what he was unsettled me. I didn't know what to listen for. I hoped and feared that he would contact me out of the other members of the group because it was my mother who had created him. He had been helping me in the Academy, but I had no idea how to hear him. So much hinged on the slight hope that we could communicate with a being none of us understood.

"He hears us."

My head lifted at the sound of Lyris' voice. The little witch looked amazed and terrified at the same time. She met my gaze, her green eyes sparking with excitement. "He's talking to me!"

I pushed down my disappointment that my mother's friend had chosen to talk to Lyris instead of me. "Ask him if he knows the chant."

"Cadish, do you know the chant?" Lyris asked.

She looked around the stairway as if she didn't know where the voice was coming from. Suddenly her head turned left. "He knows it," she said.

"What do we do?" Dara pressed.

"We need pure moonlight," Lyris said. "We'll put the moonstones in a circle and Vicken has to be inside of it."

Everyone exchanged glances.

"I'll get him," I told my team.

"Finn, you can't," Dara protested.

I nodded. "I can. I've got to." I looked at my friends. "Alden, Jean, find me something to bind him with." They disappeared up the stairs. I turned to the others. "Lyris, you and Brack head up to the corridor. Lorne, help them with the stones. The windows are already broken so there's nothing to obstruct the moonlight."

"What about us?" Kiyah asked, indicating herself and Dara.

"I'll need your help getting him upstairs." Now wasn't the time to beat around the bush. "This isn't going to be easy," I told them. "We need to be strong. Neither Vicken nor the demon are going to like this. He'll fight us every step of the way, and he's stronger than ever. But if we give up, he's lost to us."

"We're there," Kiyah said firmly. Her worry for Vicken shone bright in her light blue eyes.

"We've got this," Dara said. I felt her push reassurance at the team. If ever we needed it, now was the time.

"We found chains!" Alden called down.

They clanged as the little Grim and the vampire ran down together. A feeling of pride welled in me when I looked at our group. Any prejudice the members might have had about working together in the beginning was long gone. Vampires worked beside a warlock, the witch combined forces with the Grim, and all of them listened to a werewolf who was just beginning to understand what he could do. I couldn't help the feeling of accomplishment that filled me. If we failed, it wouldn't be for lack of heart.

Jean handed me the chains. "Good luck, Finn."

"Thanks," I replied. I looked at the others. "Don't open the door until you hear my voice. If I fail, you'll have to leave him in there until the professors come up with another option." I met Kiyah's gaze. The bite scars on her wrist matched my own. She had already sacrificed so much to save his life. I knew she wouldn't give up if Vicken bested me. "Got it?"

"Got it," the werewolf replied quietly, her gaze firm.

I put a hand on the door. "Brack, close it tight the moment I'm inside."

"How will you see?" Alden asked.

"I'm a werewolf," I told him with a grin. "Seeing in the dark is the least of my problems."

At my nod, Brack released his hold on the door. The moment it opened a crack, a massive force surged against it. My team pushed back, struggling to keep it closed.

"He's too strong!" Lorne protested.

"I'll push him back when I get through," I told them between gritted teeth as I fought to keep the door shut until we were ready. "Hold on."

I slipped the chains over my shoulder and under my other arm so that my hands were free.

"Alright, let it go just a bit," I commanded.

Dara grabbed my hand before I could move.

"Come back to me," she said. She leaned close and kissed me on the lips.

I closed my eyes for a brief second and allowed her calmness to quiet my pounding heart before I stepped back.

"I'll come back to you," I promised.

She nodded with a reluctant expression, her violet eyes filled with worry.

I crossed to the door. "Let's do this."

My team let the door open just wide enough for me to slip through. I was about to enter the door when a bony white hand shot out and grabbed my arm. The demon yanked me inside and the door shut behind us with a bang.

Chapter Sixteen

DARKNESS FILLED THE ROOM. Any hope I had that I could see was immediately dashed. It was as dark as the demon realm. Vicken's demon was comfortable.

I pushed away the fear that threatened to overcome me. I might not be able to see, but I had other senses. I crouched and listened to Vicken's breathing. The chains rattled with my movements. I was tempted to phase to fight him, but any chance I had of binding him would be gone. Phasing would have to be my last option.

"Finn."

The low, raspy voice cut straight through me. It was Vicken's to be sure, but something else colored it, something dark, twisted, and promising pain.

"Finn, I told you I would make your loved ones pay."

My lips pulled back in a snarl. "You're dead."

"On the contrary," the dark voice replied. "Your beloved professor is dead, as well as your uncle, and if you don't act soon, your weakling vampire will be soon to follow." A dark chuckle sounded, then, "Who will be next, Finn? I should have killed that empath of yours before you could rescue her. I was so close, too. Her pale skin, those purple eyes so wide in fear. She smelled simply tantalizing, Finnley."

My hands balled into fists at my sides. I ducked under the chain and wound it carefully into loops. Vicken walked around me, his steps dragging and scratching the floor. I imagined how much his clawed feet would hurt if he kicked me; the thought kept me focused and facing him as he circled.

"Your body is gone, so you took another one. You're a parasite," I said, my voice level.

"You can do better than that," Chutka taunted in Vicken's voice.

"I don't need to do better than that," I replied. I spun on one knee to keep facing him. "I don't need to best you, Chutka. You're the one who destroyed your body with your own fear. You were devoured by your own fire. That must have hurt."

A snort sounded, followed by the demon's dark chuckle. "Purity comes through sacrifice and pain. Why do you think my demons feast on fear?"

"Feasted," I corrected.

The footsteps paused. "What?"

I realized he didn't know. That brought a smile to my face. I let him hear it in my voice. "Your demons are dead, Chutka. Every last one of them. We vanquished your subordinates. You have no more followers. You're alone."

Silence filled the air. It was broken by the Demon Prince's grunt. "I don't care."

"Yes, you do," I replied. "I can hear it. No one wants to be alone. You need others to follow you." I paused, then said, "I'll follow you."

"To kill me," Chutka said with a dark chuckle. "Nice try."

I shook my head. "No. For the power." I allowed a heartbeat of silence to follow before I said, "I saw my uncle's thoughts."

"Conrad was weak," Chutka growled.

"But I'm strong," I replied. "I'm an Alpha. The Academy is full of werewolves and I know where there are more. We could start another demon army, but this time with the strength of the moon to fuel them."

I couldn't read the Demon Prince's tone when he said in Vicken's voice, "Why?"

"I told you," I replied shortly. "I want the power I felt when Conrad opened the gate. I'm tired of hiding from the world. I want to control it. I need to control it." I let my frustrations color my voice, sending the truth through my words so that he would hear it.

I had no idea if it would work, but I had to try. I could only hope that the thought of being alone would spur Chutka into recklessness. It was Vicken's only hope.

"You're tired of being weak," Chutka finally said.

"I'm not weak," I replied. "But I want to be stronger."

"You have no idea what strength is until you've felt the true nature of the demon realm," the Demon Prince said. "Take my hand. I'll show you what power really feels like."

I reached out a hand. Vicken's fingers grabbed mine as Chutka's claws sank into my wrist. Working quickly before he could react, I looped the chain around his wrist and spun around his side while still holding onto his hand.

"What are you—"

I yanked and the chain tightened behind his back, cutting off his protest.

"No!" the Demon Prince growled.

He ripped on the chain. The force flipped me onto my back. I heard the hiss of air as he kicked at me. Before the kick could land, I rolled out of the way with the chain still in my hands.

Chutka yanked on it again, which had the benefit of jerking me back to my feet. I took advantage of the momentum to climb up and over him the way Vicken had done to the Darkest Warlock. I jumped off his back, dropped to one knee, and threw the chain around his legs.

The Demon Prince caught onto what I was doing. He let out a roar and tried to swipe at me, but I ducked at the sound of the air. Before I could climb back to my feet, his foot connected with my chest and his claws punctured my skin. My breath left me in a rush as I rolled across the ground.

The sound of the chains loosening sent fear spiking through me. I leaped to my feet and grasped desperately at where it sounded the end of the chain was. The Demon Prince caught me by my throat and lifted me into the air. His claws tightened. I struggled to kick him, but he merely lifted me higher.

"You tried to trick me," he said. He raked his claws down my chest. A shout of pain escaped me. "You'll pay," he growled.

I grabbed at the chains that looped around his wrist and pulled. The end tightened around his legs and he stumbled backwards slightly. Taking advantage of his poor balance, I threw myself to the side and felt him topple with me.

The moment my feet touched the ground, I tore free from his grasp, brought his hands up the way Vicken had done to Grayson, looped his legs into the mix, and pulled the chains tight. The Demon Prince lay hogtied in the middle of the floor. I threw two more loops around his arms and legs to ensure that he was unable to move.

I rose with the chain in one hand, my muscles tense in case Chutka tried to struggle.

"What are you doing?" the Demon Prince demanded.

"Saving my friend," I replied in a growl. I turned toward the door. "Open up! It's me!"

The door immediately opened, flooding the basement in pale light.

"Finn?" Dara called.

"It's alright," I reassured them. "He's tied up. But we've got to hurry." I glared down at Chutka in Vicken's body. "The sooner we get rid of this filth, the better."

My team hurried inside. A single laugh escaped Dara at the sight.

"Vicken would be proud," she said.

"Let's hope he can tell me himself," I replied.

It took all of us to carry the Demon Prince in Vicken's body up the stairs. When we reached the corridor, we stopped at the sight of the professors and students waiting.

"What are you all doing here?" I asked in surprise.

"Helping you save him," Professor Mellon said.

"He's one of us," Espy from Mr. Seedly's class told me with a nod of her blue-feathered hair.

"Yeah, one of us," Aerlis from my second period class echoed.

Professor Rexus cleared his throat. I recognized Dr. Six's handiwork in the bandages around one of his thick horns. His deep voice echoed across the room when he said, "We are more than just a school. We are a family, and a family protects its own."

Headmistress Wrengold stepped from the crowd. "We'll do this together, Mr. Briscoe."

Students and professors alike helped to carry Chutka to the middle of the moonstone ring. The need to phase surged over me the second I neared it. I backed quickly away with the rest of my wolf pack and watched the others set the demon-possessed vampire down. The Demon Prince struggled. It was clear by the desperation in his flaming eyes that the moonlight hurt, but he couldn't break free of the chains.

"Let's begin," the Headmistress said. "Lyris, what is the chant?"

The little witch listened quietly for a few moments before raising her voice. "Witches and warlocks, repeat after me."

The words she said didn't make sense to me, but they were swiftly taken up by the others. Their voices filled the room, bouncing off the walls and the ceiling until they intertwined and crossed in a beautiful tapestry of sound.

"That's it."

I turned to see who was talking, but nobody was there.

"They've got to keep it up."

Warmth filled me at the fact that my mother's friend was talking to me.

"For how long?" I asked Cadish.

"As long as it takes. You'll know when to act."

I glanced behind me in surprise. "Act?"

"The moonlight reveals our truth," Cadish replied. "When the truth is revealed, you'll have a choice to make."

"I don't like the sound of that," I told him. "Why is there a choice?"

"There's always a choice," Cadish said elusively.

As I watched, the moonstones began to glow. A shimmering, lustrous dome appeared over Vicken. The Demon Prince struggled beneath Vicken's skin, but he couldn't get free.

"Will I know what choice to make?" I asked worriedly.

"You've always known," Cadish said.

I felt something be pressed into my hand. When I looked down, I saw Professor Brigg's walking stick. It had been cracked down the middle. Golden light glowed from the gaps in the wood.

"Break it through," Cadish told me. "Pierce their hearts. Kill them both."

I looked up to see that the chant was working. Vicken's body was being separated from the Demon Prince. In the middle, their forms still merged as though reluctant to part. Vicken's face was twisted in pain, Chutka's in determination. He would fight to destroy us all.

"Both?" I said. I shook my head. "I can't do that."

"Then you've already failed," Cadish told me. His voice faded until only a whisper met my ear. "Trust your mother."

I couldn't imagine driving half of the walking stick into Vicken's heart like a stake. Energy pulsed from the cracked wood. Numbly, I lifted it up and broke it in two. Each half was about as thick as a quarter and as long as my arm. I stared from them to the two separating bodies. The stakes warmed in my hands.

"They're almost apart!" Lyris called out. "What do we do?"

"We have to kill the Demon Prince!" the Headmistress said. "Mercer, do you have anything strong enough?"

"I don't know," the sweeper replied. He had brought a huge bag with him and was rummaging through it, but didn't looked pleased at what he found.

"We've got to hurry," Brack said, his voice tight.

"It's getting brighter!" Professor Mantis called out as she chanted with her double-jointed arms above her head. "We're going to lose the stones!"

As if on cue, one of the moonstones shattered. Gasps sounded across the room, and then another stone followed. The dome waivered.

"Mercer, it's now or never!" the Headmistress demanded.

"I-I don't have anything," the stone-faced man replied. Fear showed in his usually expressionless gaze.

"I do."

Everyone looked at me. My grip tightened on the stakes.

“When I say so, stop chanting,” I commanded.

“But they’ll lose the dome. It’s the only thing keeping Chutka at bay,” Professor Mellon said.

“I can’t enter or I’ll phase. I need the pathway to be clear,” I replied.

The Headmistress nodded. “Very well. Students, back away.” She shot me a look. “Mr. Briscoe, I hope you know what you’re doing.”

I didn’t, but there was no reason to tell her that. I crossed to the edge of the moonstone ring. From that proximity, the impulse to phase was nearly overwhelming. I watched Vicken and the Demon Prince struggle, the former to break free and the latter to hold on. Vicken’s body was Chutka’s last hope. The moment they separated, Chutka would be at his weakest.

Another stone exploded. The two forms inside the dome pulled together.

“Louder!” I yelled.

The chanting rose to an earsplitting volume. Voices shouted around me with the professors leading, desperate to protect their school. The remaining moonstones glowed so brightly I could barely see beyond them. The two bodies pulled apart, and in a split second, I saw the gap between the pair.

“Stop!” I commanded.

The voices fell away and so did the dome. The instant it was gone, I leaped inside and raised both stakes above my head.

“No, Finn!” Kiyah shouted.

“Finn, what are you doing?” I heard the Headmistress call.

“Finn, wait!” Dara pleaded.

I ignored them as I stood above Vicken’s pale form and the Demon Prince’s insubstantial one. Vicken’s eyes met mine. He gave a barely perceptible nod. It was all I needed.

I drove both stakes down as hard as I could. One pierced flesh while the other slammed through the ghostly dark form into the floor. Cries of pain came from both of them. I backed away and watched Vicken and Chutka writhe against the stakes that pinned them down. Vicken's pale hands came away bloody and dark while the Demon Prince's scrambled through the stake but were unable to grasp it.

I heard Kiyah crying behind me with Dara trying to comfort her, but I couldn't tear my gaze away from the two forms. Vicken's eyes opened one last time and he looked at me with pain in his yellow gaze.

"Thank you, Finn," he whispered.

He closed his eyes again and his head lolled to the side. At the same time, the Demon Prince gave one last shriek of pain that made everyone in the corridor cringe, then he was gone. Vicken's body lost its shape, waivered, and then vanished like Chutka's had done.

"Where is he?" Kiyah demanded.

"Where did he go?" Jean asked from my left.

"Did Finn kill him?" someone else asked.

A familiar voice broke the thick silence to say, "Finn couldn't kill me if he tried."

Stark relief flooded through me. I watched as Vicken stepped from the tear behind the moonstone circle as easily as if he was entering from another room. He appeared whole and complete instead of the battered, barely-standing vampire I had survived beside in the demon realm. Clawed tentacles and suction-padded arms reached from the crack behind him but didn't touch him.

"Brack, if you'd please," the vampire instructed.

"Gladly," the warlock replied.

Brack lifted a hand and the crack snapped shut, then vanished entirely. The reaching limbs broke off and fell writhing to the floor. I could only imagine the wails on the other side.

Vicken met my gaze. "You killed me?"

I lifted a shoulder. “I was told to trust my mother.”

He nodded. “She was a smart woman.”

“Yes, she was,” the Headmistress said from behind me.

Kiyah shook her head. “I don’t understand what just happened.” Tears glittered in her eyes. She didn’t look as though she dared to approach Vicken.

“The Vicken you saw wasn’t me,” the vampire explained. “When I bit the demon, it became a gateway for Chutka to come back. He used part of my soul and part of his own to meld a body that was both of ours. I could feel what he was doing, but I didn’t have any control. Chutka climbed through the crack and left me in the demon realm.” He shook his head. “I knew the only way to get through was for someone to destroy Chutka’s body and soul, but I didn’t know how to tell anyone.”

“That’s where I came in,” a voice said in my ear.

Vicken nodded as if he heard it, too. “Cadish found me. I was able to send Briggs’ walking stick with him. It was glowing in the darkness. The only light down there.”

I couldn’t begin to imagine how it felt sending away the only source of light he had without the reassurance that he wouldn’t be stuck there forever. The briefest glimmer of the emptiness he had felt showed in his gaze before he blinked and it was gone.

“I knew I could count on Finn,” he said, slapping my chest. He pulled his hand away to look at the blood that showed on his palm from my battle with the Demon Prince.

“Now it’s your turn to be taken care of,” the vampire told me.

“I’m fine,” I protested.

Dara ducked under my arm. “No, you’re not,” she said. “It’s time you let us handle things for a change.”

I shook my head. “That’s a horrible plan.”

Vicken grinned. “That’s why I like it.”

The moment we reached the infirmary, Dr. Six shook her head and sighed. "Stitches and sleep, that's what you need," she proclaimed.

I turned around to flee, but my friends grabbed my shoulders and forced me back. It was only through intense grumbling and protesting that I was finally able to escape with bandages, a handful of crystals to place around my bed, and the promise that I would sleep in the moonlight for the next several nights. Only Dara's reassurance that she would keep me on that strict schedule appeased the doctor's concerns.

"It's beautiful out here," Dara said quietly from my side. "And the moonlight feels great."

I looked up from the bed of blankets she had spread across a tarp on the snow near the cemetery. She sat up near the pillows looking cozy in her long, thick coat. Her heart glowed as the light of the moon revealed her empath affinity. If my body hadn't been so tired from fighting and healing, I would have been in wolf form beside her reveling in the healing light. As it was, I was content to lay there and watch the way the moonlight lingered in her hair and made her violet eyes bright.

"I think they love it here, too," she noted.

I followed her gaze to the bears that nestled under the trees on the other side of the cemetery. They had put on weight with the diet of meat scraps and bones Mr. Handsworth dolled out to them each day. Away from the Den, the bears had become as docile as puppies. It was nice to see them as carefree as I felt.

"They definitely love it here," I agreed. "And so do the dragons."

We both looked up to see the slender forms flitting and twisting around the branches and bushes in their own game. Occasionally, little puffs of brightly colored flames would light up the air only to vanish with mint, berry, and lavender scents.

"They do," Dara said. "I can feel their happiness. Especially Sparrow's. She's found her family."

As if she knew we were talking about her, the little purple and black dragon separated from the others and flew down from the trees. She landed on one of my knees and curled up into a contented ball. As I watched, her red tongue snaked out to lick the remains of whatever bug she had eaten from her face.

The other dragons drifted down as well. Dara seemed particularly pleased when a red and black one settled on her shoulder. A green and yellow one took up residence on one knee while a pink and orange one wrapped around the empath's wrist.

None of the other dragons came to me. It was as if Sparrow had claimed me for her own, and as their chosen leader, they respected her decision and settled onto the blankets instead.

"We've been on quiet the journey," I said. I ran a finger down the little dragon's back, then turned to look at the gravestone where she had chosen to stay with me instead of going with Alden to the next life.

The new tombstone beside Mezania's gleamed in the moonlight. The name Trace Nathaniel Briggs showed in stark contrast to the marble. All across the face of the white stone, students had written the things they had learned from the professor. Notes like, 'To never be late' and 'Electricity is scary' paled next to my handwriting. The words, 'Why cats land on their feet', stood out in the bright blue ink Lyris had made for me. Next to the words, I had drawn a rough sketch. It was of a human holding hands with a ghost. Below it was written the words I had overheard Briggs tell the girl he loved who had been taken from him too soon.

"I want to live where you live, even if that means we're both ghosts."

Below that, Alden had written, "They are together in the beautiful beyond."

Past the two tombstones stood another new addition to the cemetery. The name Conrad Justin Roe was followed by an engraving of a dark-coated wolf. It watched the cemetery with calm golden eyes, a silent sentry guarding the realm he had fought so hard to protect.

"So what's next?" Dara asked, bringing my thoughts back to the present.

"Next?" I replied.

She nodded. "For Finnley Briscoe, the werewolf daredevil who slew a thousand demons and rescued the girl who loved him."

"The girl he loved," I replied, pulling her close. "There's a difference."

She smiled at me. "It's one and the same." She rested her head on my shoulder.

I slipped my fingers through hers and lifted our hands to study the way they matched up.

"The Maes are slaying the rest of the demons that were in our world before Chutka died," I said.

Dara nodded. "So no more major enemies, for now."

"For now," I agreed. "And Vicken is learning how to cope with a werewolf girlfriend."

Dara laughed. "Who would have thought?"

"Definitely not me," I said with an answering laugh. "And certainly not him. But he's really smitten."

She smiled and it was beautiful in the moonlight. "Yes, he is."

"So I guess the next big adventure is the students," I told her.

She leaned back to look at me. "The students?"

I nodded. "The Headmistress approved my syllabus for next year. I'm thinking of starting with a riddle, something Professor Briggs would approve of."

Dara smiled. "Something about cats?"

I chuckled. "Something like that."

She leaned her head back on my shoulder and I rested my chin in her hair. There would be plenty to do tomorrow, but for that moment, with the moonlight around us and the love of my life in my arms, it was enough to simply be.

About the Author

Cheree Alsop is an award-winning, best-selling author who has published over 45 books. She is the mother of a beautiful, talented daughter and amazing twin sons who fill every day with joy and laughter. She is married to her best friend, Michael, the light of her life and her soulmate who shares her dreams and inspires her by reading the first drafts and giving much appreciated critiques. Cheree works as a fulltime author and mother, which is more play than work! She enjoys reading, traveling to tropical beaches, riding motorcycles, spending time with her wonderful children, and going on family adventures while planning her next book.

Cheree and Michael live in Utah where they rock out, enjoy the outdoors, plan great quests, and never stop dreaming.

You can find Cheree's other books at
www.chereealsop.com

REVIEWS

The Girl from the Stars Series

This is my favorite Cheree Alsop book now! Her best yet! I loved it. So many twists and turns, great characters, excitement and hints of romance. I can't wait for the next one in the series.

—Voca Matisse, Reviewer

Fantastic book! Cheree's ability to write an amazing character that you not only sympathize with but also grow to care for, is one of the fabulous writing abilities that she lends to every story. This story line was full of epic twists and wry humor that had me engaged the entire way through. All in all a fun enjoyable read.

—akgodwin, Amazon Reviewer

This was one of the best books I have read in a while. Sci-fi, adventure, thriller... could not put the book away. I already bought the second book in the series, and hope the third will come out soon.

—Kindle Customer

The main character, Liora, is a very mixed up but emerging person who is a genetic mutt! Half of her DNA is totally violence oriented whilst the other half is straight human, which is to say violent when necessary but basically well rounded. In the beginning she was a slave in a circus and had never known anyone she could trust or care for, and even when she is rescued from that hell she has a hard time adjusting to the idea that she can fit in anywhere. The action is frequent and well written and over time she keeps trying to both find reasons to fit in and reasons to strike out on her own. This is not resolved in the first book, and makes you want to read more. I like the series a lot and hope the writer keeps them coming.

—Sam, Amazon Reviewer

Dr Wolf, the Fae Rift Series

Dr. Wolf, the Fae Rift Series Book 1- Shockwave by Cheree Alsop is a movie transcript ready and suspensefully alluring tale that weaves the mind of the reader around the world of wild dreams.

— Rachel Anderson, Amazon Reviewer

Wow! Was not expecting enjoying this book as much as I did. Ms. Alsop had me drawn in front the get go. The writing was fantastic, the story just flowed so easily and I could not put the book down. I enjoyed all the characters and love her imagination. The banter with the characters had me laughing out loud (I love the fairy and the vampire). I really enjoyed the storyline and the whole what if of falling into a rift. I would highly recommend this book to anyone looking for a nice fresh look on paranormal.

— Amazon Verified Reviewer

Demon Spiral picks up right where Shockwave left off...Once again, I could not put this book down. The flow of the story is amazing and the banter that the author was able to put into the book just made for a very enjoyable read. I highly recommend Cheree Alsop and look forward to reading the next in this series as well.

—Crystal's Review, GoodReads Reviewer

I had to download the sample for this because I was sure I wanted it. I bought the book after the first page. It's almost like Dr. Who with Fae.

—Chris Hughes, Amazon Reviewer

The Silver Series

"Cheree Alsop has written *Silver* for the YA reader who enjoys both werewolves and coming-of-age tales. Although I don't fall into this demographic, I still found it an entertaining read on a long plane trip! The author has put a great deal of thought into balancing a tale that could apply to any teen (death of a parent, new school, trying to find one's place in the world) with the added spice of a youngster dealing with being exceptionally different from those around him, and knowing that puts him in danger."

—Robin Hobb, author of the Farseer Trilogy

"I honestly am amazed this isn't absolutely EVERYWHERE! Amazing book. Could NOT put it down! After reading this book, I purchased the entire series!"

—Josephine, Amazon Reviewer

"A page-turner that kept me wide awake and wanting more. Great characters, well written, tenderly developed, and thrilling. I loved this book, and you will too."

—Valerie McGilvrey

"Super glad that I found this series! I am crushed that it is at its end. I am sure we will see some of the characters in the next series, but it just won't be the same. I am 41 years old, and am only a little embarrassed to say I was crying at 3 a.m. this morning while finishing the last book. Although this is a YA series, all ages will enjoy the Silver Series. Great job by Cheree Alsop. I am excited to see what she comes up with next."

—Jennc, Amazon Reviewer

The Werewolf Academy Series

If you love werewolves, paranormal, and looking for a book like House of Night or Vampire Academy this is it! YA for sure.

—Reviewer for Sweets Books

I got this book from a giveaway, and it's one of the coolest books I have ever read. If you love Hogwarts, and Vampire Academy, or basically anything that has got to do with supernatural people studying, this is the book for you.

—Maryam Dinzly

This series is truly a work of art, sucked in immediately and permanently. The first line and you are in the book. Cheree Alsop is a gifted writer, all of her books are my complete favorites!! This series has to be my absolute favorite, Alex is truly a wonderful character who I so wish was real so I can meet him and thank him. Once you pick this book up you won't put it down till it's finished. A must read!!!!!

—BookWolf Brianna

Listed with Silver Moon as the top most emotional of Cheree's books, I loved Instinct for its raw truth about the pain, the heartbreak, and the guilt that Alex fights.

—Loren Weaver

Great story. Loaded with adventure at every turn. Can't wait till the next book. Very enjoyable, light reading. I would recommend to all young and old readers.

—Sharon Klein

The Galdoni Series

"This is absolutely one of the best books I have ever read in my life! I loved the characters and their personalities, the storyline and the way it was written. The bravery, courage and sacrifice that Kale showed was amazing and had me scolding myself to get a grip and stop crying! This book had adventure, romance and comedy all rolled into one terrific book I LOVED the lesson in this book, the struggles that the characters had to go through (especially the forbidden love)...I couldn't help wondering what it would be like to live among such strangely beautiful creatures that acted, at times, more caring and compassionate than the humans. Overall, I loved this book...I recommend it to ANYONE who fancies great books."

—iBook Reviewer

"I was not expecting a free novel to beat anything that I have ever laid eyes upon. This book was touching and made me want more after each sentence."

—Sears1994, iBook Reviewer

"This book was simply heart wrenching. It was an amazing book with a great plot. I almost cried several times. All of the scenes were so real it felt like I was there witnessing everything."

—Jeanine Drake, iBook Reveiwer

"Galdoni is an amazing book; it is the first to actually make me cry! It is a book that really touches your heart, a romance novel that might change the way you look at someone. It did that to me."

—Coralee2, Reviewer

"Wow. I simply have no words for this. I highly recommend it to anyone who stumbled across this masterpiece. In other words, READ IT!"

—Troublecat101, iBook Reviewer

The Monster Asylum Series

What a rollercoaster, wow!! I never ever cried when reading a vampire book, but I did this time. I must say it's the best vampire book I've read since ever. One of the best books ever read so far.

—Conny, Goodreads Reviewer

I downloaded this book because of Cheree, I love her imagination. This one is so much fun to read; once I started I couldn't put it down. And now I believe not all Monsters are bad!! Looking forward to the next book in the series. Thanks Cheree

—Doughgirl61, Amazon Reviewer

Keeper of the Wolves

"This is without a doubt the VERY BEST paranormal romance/adventure I have ever read and I've been reading these types of books for over 45 years. Excellent plot, wonderful protagonists—even the evil villains were great. I read this in one sitting on a Saturday morning when there were so many other things I should have been doing. I COULD NOT put it down! I also appreciated the author's research and insights into the behavior of wolf packs. I will CERTAINLY read more by this author and put her on my 'favorites' list."

—N. Darisse

"This is a novel that will emotionally cripple you. Be sure to keep a box of tissues by your side. You will laugh, you will cry, and you will fall in love with Keeper. If you loved *Black Beauty* as a child, then you will truly love *Keeper of the Wolves* as an adult. Put this on your 'must read' list."

—Fortune Ringquist

"Cheree Alsop mastered the mind of a wolf and wrote the most amazing story I've read this year. Once I started, I couldn't stop reading. Personal needs no longer existed. I turned the last page with tears streaming down my face."

—Rachel Andersen, Amazon Reviewer

"I just finished this book. Oh my goodness, did I get emotional in some spots. It was so good. The courage and love portrayed is amazing. I do recommend this book. Thought provoking."

—Candy, Amazon Reviewer

Thief Prince

"I absolutely loved this book! I could not put it down. . . The Thief Prince will whisk you away into a new world that you will not want to leave! I hope that Ms. Alsop has more about this story to write, because I would love more Kit and Andric! This is one of my favorite books so far this year! Five Stars!"

—Crystal, Book Blogger at Books are Sanity

". . . Once I started I couldn't put it down. The story is amazing. The plot is new and the action never stops. The characters are believable and the emotions presented are beautiful and real. If anyone wants a good, clean, fun, romantic read, look no further. I hope there will be more books set in Debria, or better yet, Antor."

—SH Writer, Amazon Reviewer

"This book was a roller coaster of emotions: tears, laughter, anger, and happiness. I absolutely fell in love with all of the characters placed throughout this story. This author knows how to paint a picture with words."

—Kathleen Vales

"Awesome book! It was so action packed, I could not put it down, and it left me wanting more! It was very well written, leaving me feeling like I had a connection with the characters."

—M. A., Amazon Reviewer

The Shadows Series

"This was a heart-warming tale of rags to riches. It was also wonderfully described and the characters were vivid and vibrant; a story that teaches of love defying boundaries and of people finding acceptance."

—Sara Phillip, Book Reviewer

"This is the best book I have ever had the pleasure of reading. . . It literally has everything, drama, action, fighting, romance, adventure, & suspense. . . Nexa is one of the most incredible female protagonists ever written. . .It literally had me on pins & needles the ENTIRE time. . . I cannot recommend this book highly enough. Please give yourself a wonderful treat & read this book… you will NOT be disappointed!!!"

—Jess- Goodreads Reviewer

"Took my breath away; excitement, adventure and suspense. . . This author has extracted a tender subject and created a supernatural fantasy about seeing beyond the surface of an individual. . . Also the romantic scenes would make a girl swoon. . . The fights between allies and foes and blood lust would attract the male readers. . .The conclusion was so powerful and scary this reader was sitting on the edge of her seat."

—Susan Mahoney, Book Blogger

"Adventure, incredible amounts of imagination and description go into this world! It is a buy now, don't leave the couch until the last chapter has reached an end kind of read!"

—Malcay- Amazon Reviewer

"The high action tale with the underlying love story that unfolds makes you want to keep reading and not put it down. I can't wait until the next book in the Shadows Series comes out."

—Karen- Amazon Reviewer

". . . It's refreshing to see a female character portrayed without the girly clichés most writers fall into. She is someone I would like to meet in real life, and it is nice to read the first person POV of a character who is so well-round that she is brave, but still has the softer feminine side that defines her character. A definite must read."

—S. Teppen- Goodreads Reviewer

The Small Town Superhero Series

"A very human superhero- Cheree Alsop has written a great book for youth and adults alike. Kelson, the superhero, is battling his own demons plus bullies in this action packed narrative. Small Town Superhero had me from the first sentence through the end. I felt every sorrow, every pain and the delight of rushing through the dark on a motorcycle. Descriptions in Small Town Superhero are so well written the reader is immersed in the town and lives of its inhabitants."

—Rachel Andersen, Book Reviewer

"Anyone who grew up in a small town or around motorcycles will love this! It has great characters and flows well with martial arts fighting and conflicts involved."

—Karen, Amazon Reviewer

"Fantastic story...and I love motorcycles and heroes who don't like the limelight. Excellent character development. You'll like this series!"

—Michael, Amazon Reviewer

"Another great read; couldn't put it down. Would definitely recommend this book to friends and family. She has put out another great read. Looking forward to reading more!"

—Benton Garrison, Amazon Reviewer

"I enjoyed this book a lot. Good teen reading. Most books I read are adult contemporary; I needed a change and this was a good change. I do recommend reading this book! I will be looking out for more books from this author. Thank you!"

—Cass, Amazon Reviewer

Stolen

"This book will take your heart, make it a little bit bigger, and then fill it with love. I would recommend this book to anyone from 10-100. To put this book in words is like trying to describe love. I had just gotten it and I finished it the next day because I couldn't put it down. If you like action, thrilling fights, and/or romance, then this is the perfect book for you."

—Steven L. Jagerhorn

"Couldn't put this one down! Love Cheree's ability to create totally relatable characters and a story told so fluidly you actually believe it's real."

—Sue McMillin, Amazon Reviewer

"I enjoyed this book it was exciting and kept you interested. The characters were believable. And the teen romance was cute."

—Book Haven- Amazon Reviewer

"I really liked this book . . . I was pleasantly surprised to discover this well-written book. . .I'm looking forward to reading more from this author."

—Julie M. Peterson- Amazon Reviewer

"Great book! I enjoyed this book very much it keeps you wanting to know more! I couldn't put it down! Great read!"

—Meghan- Amazon Reviewer

"A great read with believable characters that hook you instantly. . . I was left wanting to read more when the book was finished."

—Katie- Goodreads Reviewer

Heart of the Wolf

"Absolutely breathtaking! This book is a roller coaster of emotions that will leave you exhausted!!! A beautiful fantasy filled with action and love. I recommend this book to all fantasy lovers and those who enjoy a heartbreaking love story that rivals that of Romeo and Juliet. I couldn't put this book down!"

—Amy May

"What an awesome book! A continual adventure, with surprises on every page. What a gifted author she is. You just can't put the book down. I read it in two days. Cheree has a way of developing relationships and pulling at your heart. You find yourself identifying with the characters in her book...True life situations make this book come alive for you and gives you increased understanding of your own situation in life. Magnificent story and characters. I've read all of Cheree's books and recommend them all to you...especially if you love adventures."

—Michael, Amazon Reviewer

"You'll like this one and want to start part two as soon as you can! If you are in the mood for an adventure book in a faraway kingdom where there are rival kingdoms plotting and scheming to gain more power, you'll enjoy this novel. The characters are well developed, and of course with Cheree there is always a unique supernatural twist thrown into the story as well as romantic interests to make the pages fly by."

Karen, Amazon Reviewer

When Death Loved an Angel

"This style of book is quite a change for this author so I wasn't expecting this, but I found an interesting story of two very different souls who stepped outside of their "accepted roles" to find love and forgiveness, and what is truly of value in life and death."

—Karen, Amazon Reviewer

"When Death Loved an Angel by Cheree Alsop is a touching paranormal romance that cranks the readers' thinking mode into high gear."

—Rachel Andersen, Book Reviewer

"Loved this book. I would recommend this book to everyone. And be sure to check out the rest of her books, too!"

—Malcay, Book Reviewer

The Million Dollar Gift

...This was a very beautiful, heart warming story about a young man who finds love, and family again on Christmas. I really enjoyed this short story. It truly inspires the meaning of Christmas in my eyes. It was utterly beautiful, and I highly recommend it. The plot is very interesting, and the characters catch your heart and lead on this very sad and happy story.

—Whitney@Shooting Stars Review

I recommend The Million Dollar Gift as a way to remember what Christmas is about: Love. Family. Friendship. Because a life without love isn't really worth living anyway.

—Loren Weaver

When Chase risks his life to save a brother and sister just before Christmas, his life becomes entwined with theirs more intricately than he could have imagined. Emotional and moving, this is a story of a young man whose troubled heart is tested by the one thing he is unprepared to face, love. MY TAKE- This is a fast, fun, emotional Christmas read. Made me cry.

—Donna Weaver

Never stop dreaming!

25179927R00139

Printed in Poland
by Amazon Fulfillment
Poland Sp. z o.o., Wrocław